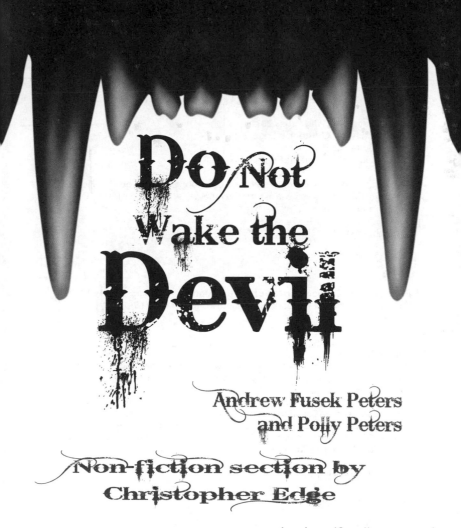

Do Not Wake the Devil

Andrew Fusek Peters
and Polly Peters

Non-fiction section by
Christopher Edge

Part of Pearson

Heinemann is an imprint of Pearson Education Limited, Edinburgh Gate, Harlow, Essex, CM20 2JE.

www.pearsonschoolsandfecolleges.co.uk

Heinemann is a registered trademark of Pearson Education Limited

Text © Andrew and Polly Peters 2011
Non-fiction text © Christopher Edge
Typeset by Kamae Design
Cover design by Wooden Ark Studios

The rights of Andrew and Polly Peters and Christopher Edge to be identified as authors of this work have been asserted by them in accordance with the Copyright, Designs and Patents Act 1988.

First published 2011

14 13 12 11 10
10 9 8 7 6 5 4 3 2 1

British Library Cataloguing in Publication Data
A catalogue record for this book is available from the British Library

ISBN 978 0 435 04599 9

Printed at Henry Ling, UK

Acknowledgements

We would like to thank the following school and students for their invaluable help in the development and trialling of this book:

Biggar High School, South Lanarkshire

Sean Christie, Andrew Colgan, Daniel Cummings, Nathan Gallant, Aaron Houston, Rachel Inglis, Stephen Lamberton, Struan MacDonald, Katie McAndrew, Isla McLachlan, Darren Riddell, Tiegan Ritchie, Danielle White, David Whitefield.

CONTENTS

Non-fiction:

CHAPTER 1

Sunday night, four days before midsummer

Arthur jolted round in fear. 'Did you hear that?' he whispered.

'What?' said Yaz.

'Growling. Like a tiger or something.'

Yaz punched Arthur's arm. 'What are you – *a scaredy cat*? Since when did Shropshire have tigers, huh?'

They were perched on the Devil's Chair – a huge outcrop of rock right at the top of a hill called the Stiperstones. Under the three-quarter moon and the fading dusk, they could see the valleys and hills spread out around them. Their village was already hidden by a thick summer fog.

There was another sudden sound. It was a deep rumble, bigger than the purr of a cat. Much bigger. 'Listen!' he said, peering into the dark shadows around them. 'I swear I heard something!'

'Yeah, yeah. Probably an owl … or a tractor,' said Yaz. 'You worry too much …' She broke off and looked at her best mate: his mess of sandy brown hair, his lanky legs and his arms almost too long for his clothes. With everything that had happened recently, she thought it was no surprise that he was getting himself into such a state.

1

But then the sound was gone. The feeling of dread left Arthur. Now he was simply sitting on a pile of stones at the top of a hill, hanging out with his mate, Yaz, while darkness fell. Arthur found himself breathing slowly again.

'Have the police said anything else?'

Arthur tried to ignore the goosebumps on his arms. 'What? Sorry, Yaz. I'm all over the place. No, nothing new. But I keep thinking. I mean, my dad knew how to look after himself, yeah?'

'Course he did, Artie,' Yaz said.

'He'd swum in that lake loads of times. He knew it really well …' Arthur trailed off because he didn't want to say what he was *really* thinking: that the one time his dad had gone swimming without Arthur, he hadn't come back. He kept going over and over it in his head, wanting to change the moment he'd said 'no thanks' to joining his dad. It had been the perfect evening for a swim in the old quarry lake, but Arthur had only wanted to play his new Xbox game. It had just come out: King Arthur and his knights taking on the bad guys with a bunch of great weapons. It had tons of 3-D gore and enough flying intestines to keep a boy happy for hours. At first, he hadn't even noticed when his dad didn't return that evening. Later, the police had sent divers down to dredge the pool. Nothing. All they could say was that there were underground rivers that fed into the lake, and that his dad could be anywhere under the hills. *Missing* was the word they used. *Disappeared.* Arthur couldn't bring himself to think about the final word. *Dead.*

'I'm sorry,' Yaz said. In four short weeks, she'd watched Arthur slowly fall apart. He didn't reply and they both fell silent.

'You know why this is called the Devil's Chair?' Yaz changed the subject quickly, hoping to take Arthur's mind off his dad for a moment.

'Course I do. But tell me again …' Arthur was cold and uncomfortable, sitting on hard stone. But the thought of going home to his weeping mum was too much right now.

'OK. Well, supposedly, the Devil was knackered after walking all the way across Wales.' When Yaz talked, her brown eyes lit up. With her spiky, dark hair and black eyeliner, she looked like she should have been singing in a band rather than hanging out in the middle of nowhere. 'Anyway, the Devil had this apron, full of rocks that he was going to dump in the River Severn, down over there.' She pointed behind her.

'And tell me, dear Yaz, why was that?' Arthur smiled for the first time that night. Everyone round here grew up with this story.

'Oh, he fancied a spot of mass murder. You know, chuck the rocks in the river, make it flood and then watch the little people scream as they get swept away.'

'Right. So not a nice bloke, the Devil.'

'Exactly. But it turns out, as he was striding over the hills, he was so tired he tripped over. The apron strings snapped, rocks fell everywhere and – hey presto – that's how we get this place!'

Arthur looked around. Under the moon, the tumble of white quartzite rocks spilled out over the hillside. 'Kind of makes sense.'

'Yeah, then the Devil had a sulky fit cos he'd stubbed his toe. Stamped his feet in a massive tantrum and crushed the huge rocks into smaller ones. Finally, he sat down and got out his pipe to have a smoke.'

'And that's why when it's foggy up here. They say it's the Devil sitting in his chair of stones, smoking his pipe …' Arthur finished. 'Speaking of which, here it comes!'

While they'd been talking, the fog from the valley behind them had crept up and now it was rolling in fast.

'That's not good,' said Yaz, frowning and jumping up. 'Better get going.'

As she darted away, the moon vanished and the view was swiftly blotted out.

'Blimey. Where are you, Yaz?'

'Right here, you idiot!' The voice was muffled. Arthur stood and stumbled towards it. All he could see was a lumpy greyness that swallowed any sound of footsteps.

Then suddenly the ground rumbled. Arthur's thoughts spun. No, that wasn't right. Since when did rocks *growl*?

'Yaz!' he cried.

No answer. Just a shape peeling away from the fog.

'Is that you? Why are you crawling?'

It was the wrong question to ask. A pair of eyes loomed right in front of him. They glittered green. Not the green of summer grass but of foaming bile. And there was a stench of rotten meat too.

'Wha– Y-Yaz?' he stuttered.

'Over here!' came a voice to his far right.

Arthur tried to back away from the shape in front of him. 'You're not Yaz!' he said, aware of how stupid he sounded.

The shadow advanced through the silent fog. The dark outline was cat-shaped. But this cat was bigger and blacker than any pet. The fog briefly gave way.

'Oh dear!' he whispered to himself. *Oh dear* was a pretty big understatement. Jaws dropped open, revealing teeth whiter than the moon. The creature crouched and Arthur could only stare.

Yaz's words came back to him. *Since when did Shropshire have tigers?* She was right. This was no tiger. It was more like the fully grown black panther he'd once seen in a zoo – and it was watching him.

The cat's shoulders dropped and sharp claws shot out from its padded paws. It was going to pounce. Any moment now Arthur would be ripped up like a sheet of paper.

CHAPTER 2

The fog was damp, covering Arthur's clothes in beads of wetness. What could he do? Scream? Run? The cat's eyes drilled into him and its sleek body was now obscured by the fog. Arthur tried not to think about teeth sinking into flesh.

'*Where is it?*' a voice hissed.

'What?' Arthur looked round, wondering who was speaking to him.

'*Where is it, boy?*' The voice was low and rasping.

Arthur was in shock. Impossible! A speaking cat? He was definitely dreaming.

Without warning, the cat flew through the air. Its claws were going to slice Arthur into salami. He should have felt fear, but in that frozen moment he only hoped that death would be quick. Maybe he'd even meet his dad on the other side.

This was it.

Whoomph! And then he was falling backwards in slow motion. His feet slipped and the rocks beneath him rammed into his back and head. The creature was on him, claws digging in like garden forks, ready to rip out his heart. And the smell from the beast's mouth was foul. A trickle of sick rose in Arthur's throat.

BANG! There was an almighty thump and a huge weight collapsed on to him. It took a second for Arthur to work out that he was still alive.

'Help!' he whimpered. 'I'm trapped. Help!'

'*Mmmf*. Don't move!'

'Yaz? Is that you?'

'Yup.' She gave a grunt and the deadweight of the beast began to shift a little. 'On the count of three, now give it some welly! One, two, three …'

Arthur's arms were trapped by his side and he could hardly breathe. But he managed a tiny sideways roll. It was just enough. He felt the weight slide off and then he was being pulled to his feet. He staggered upright and clung on to Yaz's arm.

'You … saved me … there,' he gasped, trying to get air back into his lungs.

'Yeah. Guess I did. Useful things these stones.' Yaz cradled one of the white lumps of quartzite, but Arthur noticed that her hand was trembling.

'Not … bad … for a girl.'

'Yeah. I'll pretend you didn't say that.'

They looked at each other, knowing how crazy this all was and that they were both trying to cover it by sounding normal.

'What now?' Arthur was trying to steady his breathing. 'Do you reckon it's dead?' He didn't want to step near enough to prod the lifeless body.

'Hope so. Seeing as it was about to rip you to bits, I didn't exactly give it a *little* tap on the head!'

But at the same moment, a high mewing sound escaped the cat and its body gave a long shudder. Then it twitched and lifted its head.

Yaz and Arthur shared a look of pure panic.

Arthur could barely get his words out. 'I-it's moving! Let's –'

'Run?' Yaz pushed Arthur forward. 'Like, right NOW!'

The animal was still dazed. Arthur hoped that would buy them a few precious moments. They scrambled, slithered and fell over the rocks, heading downhill. At least the fog had cleared and the moon was on their side. It lit up the path between the stones. However, their bikes were a long way down, near the bottom. Yaz was much shorter than Arthur, but her cross-country running skills saw her bounding ahead like a mountain goat. He could hardly keep up, but fear drove him on.

Arthur had often laughed with his mates at local tales of a big black cat in the hills. More like wild imagination he'd reckoned, or childish gossip.

But *this* was no silly gossip. He could hear stones rattling behind them. The beast was close, and getting closer. Then another sound cracked open the night – a strange, yowling scream

'Don't stop!' Yaz panted. 'Not far now!'

Arthur couldn't breathe. His heart hammered. His legs felt like they were full of wet sand. He couldn't do this. The larger rocks gave way to smaller stones, but there was still some way to go before the path widened out down towards the car park.

Arthur glanced back – a mistake. He saw a shadow flowing gracefully over the rocks, like oil. It was gaining on them with every heartbeat. Arthur flung himself forward, each atom of his body focused on driving him forward. The stones underfoot were like gravel now, slippery and uneven. There was the stile in the fence straight ahead. But even as he raced towards it, his feet lost their grip. His arms flapped uselessly and he was down. *Thud! Crunch!* Over and over he tumbled, his mouth full of grass and grit and blood. He was rolling like a pebble and he couldn't stop.

'Owww!' Arthur's knee smacked into the wooden post of the stile and he came to a dead stop. He wanted to lie still, but instinct kicked in. He dragged himself upright and threw himself over the stile. Yaz was ahead of him. Together, they leapt on to their bikes. Surely wheels had to be faster than four legs? Arthur hoped so. He stood on his pedals and willed the bike forward. The wheels bit into dust and finally gripped the tarmac.

But Yaz was not so lucky. Her wheel hit a rut and the bike began to spin away from her. She swore under her breath as she heard the beast fly over the fence and land right behind her.

'Come on!' screamed Arthur.

Yaz concentrated. She just had to get the pedal in the right place, push down hard and … go! Her bike shot forward. At exactly the same moment, a searing pain slashed across her right shoulder.

'No!' The bike wobbled, but Yaz held on grimly and stared straight ahead. The cat had pounced, catching her shoulder as it just missed its target. She heard an angry, spitting snarl as she managed to keep her balance and pedalled hard. Then, in a rush of speed, all she could hear was the wind in her ears as she raced after Arthur and away into the night.

Ten minutes later, they came to a screeching halt at the edge of the village.

Arthur peered round nervously. The road that wound its way back up towards the hill was empty. Nothing lurked in the shadows except the night itself.

'Are you all right?' he gasped. 'That was close … Yaz?'

'Don't … feel so good. That … thing scratched me.' She touched her shoulder. Her T-shirt was stuck to her skin and a dark, wet stain spread down her arm and dripped on to the road.

'You're bleeding! Yaz, what happened back there?'

But Yaz didn't reply. She swayed briefly, then slowly toppled sideways off her bike.

CHAPTER 3

An hour later, Yaz was fast asleep in the spare bedroom of Arthur's house. Although she only lived ten minutes away, she'd been too groggy to get home. Her mum had rushed over as soon as Arthur had rung, and the doctor had been called. The doctor had diagnosed 'shock and exhaustion' and had said sleep would be the best cure. So they had not tried to get her up again. In any case, Arthur and Yaz had grown up together and his house was like a second home for her.

In the kitchen, Arthur cupped his mug of sweet, milky tea while his mum paced up and down. Doctor Evans sat on the other side of the table, frowning and fiddling with her glasses.

'And Arthur, you say that this so-called *big cat* attacked your friend?' asked the doctor.

'I've told you already. Why don't you believe me?'

The doctor turned to his mother. 'Mrs Hatfield, I think your son is in shock too. Why these teenagers feel the need to scare themselves silly with superstitious tales I don't know.'

'And what were you doing up there on a Sunday night? You've got school tomorrow.' Arthur's mother looked worn. In the last month, grey hairs had suddenly speckled her head and now *this*.

'Would you rather we both hung around the village being loud and causing trouble?' Arthur was furious. His mates from school were OK, but spending every evening sitting in the bus shelter watching life go by was not his idea of fun.

'No,' said his mum, 'I …'

'The point is,' Doctor Evans interrupted, 'the girl probably did disturb some sort of wandering local pet and the animal lashed out in fear. Though the scratches are rather large. Hmmm …' She reached down to close her briefcase. 'The tetanus shot is just for safety's sake. Sleep is the best medicine.'

Once the doctor left, Arthur made his way upstairs.

'Wait,' said his mother. 'Sorry I snapped at you.'

'I wanted to get up high, breathe some fresh air,' answered Arthur.

'I know. You miss him so much, don't you?' There were tears in her eyes.

Arthur wanted to hug her, but he couldn't. 'Yeah,' he mumbled. 'Night, Mum.'

The next morning on the bus-ride to school, Yaz was silent next to him. She'd gotten up really early and said she felt fine. She refused to let Arthur's mum drive her. Instead, she'd got on her bike and pedalled home for breakfast.

'You all right?' said Arthur.

'My shoulder throbs a bit. That's all. Everything feels like a dream. Maybe it was.'

'It wasn't.' Arthur leaned in closer. He didn't want any of the others to hear. 'That *thing* spoke to me.'

'I think your ears have gone funny again.'

'No. Seriously. It asked me, "Where is it?"'

'Right. So, I get attacked by a panther or overgrown kitty, but first it sits down and has a chat with you – before I clobber it! And what is this "it" anyway? Some treasure or devilish weapon?' she snorted.

'How should I know? I'm just telling you what I heard.' He shoved his hands in his pockets and looked away. The bus turned at the crossroads and into the car park of Priestcastle Secondary School.

Yaz stood up then grabbed hold of the seat in front. Her face blanced.

'Hey!' said Arthur, half-joking. 'Don't go getting rabies! Frothing at the mouth is so out of fashion!'

'Thanks, Artie. With mates like you, who needs enemies? Let's just forget about last night, shall we?'

Mr Stockheart was a pretty cool teacher. His geography lessons didn't bother with rainfall patterns in Brazil. He was far more interested in the landscape around them.

'Think you're safe, here in class, in school, in this town?' he started. 'Stamp your feet three times please.'

This was a good excuse for everyone to go wild, making enough noise to shake the whole building.

'Thank you. I think we get the point!' The smile on his face was friendly but steely. They all understood the message; nobody messed with Mr Stockheart. 'Right underneath your feet is a fault line in the Earth, a stress-point between tectonic plates. It's called the Pontesford–Linley fault. Earthquakes –' here he paused and looked slowly at his class – 'don't just happen on the news far away. Of course you lot weren't even born when we had the last quake in 1990. Buildings shook, a couple of barn roofs fell in. It was a 5.1 on the Richter scale. There are machines that can read and then predict these events. And they are saying that the Earth has been grumbling again recently, so … BEWARE!'

As Mr Stockheart yelled out the last word, a boy who had been secretly texting jumped up in alarm. His phone flew through the air and smashed against a wall.

'My dear Lee!' said Mr Stockheart. 'Though mobiles are not allowed in school, I shall let you off punishment seeing as you are learning *why* they are not allowed.' He motioned the sulky boy to pick up the shattered pieces.

'Now that the rest of you have recovered,' he continued, 'let me introduce you to a new member of class, Jack Mytton.

He and his father have recently moved up here. I hope that you and the rest of Year Eight will make him welcome.'

Thirty pairs of eyes turned to the back of the room. Somehow, nobody had noticed the new boy. He raised his head and glanced coolly round the class.

Arthur had never seen anyone with hair so black. The boy wore it shoulder length. His face was pale white, two dark eyebrows meeting in the middle. And under his white school shirt, anyone could see he had serious muscles. Instead of speaking, the boy lifted his hand, like a prince greeting his subjects.

Who does he think he is? thought Arthur, staring. The rest of the class turned back. They had already lost interest.

Then the boy did something strange. He put his right thumb against his upper teeth and flicked it in the direction of Arthur. Nobody else saw.

Last week in English, Arthur remembered, Mrs C. had been talking about the first fight scene in *Romeo and Juliet*. She'd explained about old insults. *I bite my thumb at you*, she told them, was the same as certain popular swear words.

Arthur hadn't even met this new guy before. It was hardly the best way to make friends.

The boy smirked and stared at Arthur. What was he supposed to do? Give him the finger? Arthur's palms were suddenly sweaty. *Hang on a moment!* thought Arthur. *Those eyes …* It looked like the boy was wearing coloured contact lenses. Either that, or his eyes really were *that* green.

CHAPTER 4

*Monday afternoon, three days
before midsummer*

Arthur's mother was fussing round the kitchen table,
cutting slices of fruit pie and pouring tea. She had made the
effort to comb her hair and put on lipstick. At the head of
the table, in his father's chair, sat a stranger.

'Artie,' said his mum, 'I'd like you to meet Gabriel. I think
you've already met his son, Jack.'

Arthur had only just come in. Frowning, he held out his
hand and found his fingers being gripped tightly by the man.

'The pleasure is mine. Christina has told me so much
about you!'

Gabriel's slender figure was dressed in a sharp, black
suit that didn't belong in the countryside. He didn't look at
all like his son. He was thinner, with light red hair and clear
blue eyes.

Arthur instantly hated him. What was he doing here?

'Good question!' said Gabriel.

'What?' Arthur hadn't said anything.

The polite, pale face faltered for a moment. 'I mean, you
must be wondering what I am doing here? As I told your
delightful mother … I have just moved into the village –

to Fall Hall. Turns out that my ancestors came from round here. The old house is still in the family, though it's been empty for ages. We Myttons go way back. Right now I work as a consultant in the aviation industry. Flying takes me all over the world.' He paused and his eyes grew suddenly distant. 'Which means that I cannot always be around to look after my boy. I do understand that, due to very unfortunate recent events, Christina here could do with some extra work. So I have asked if she could take on a bit of housekeeping at my place when I'm away.'

Christina jumped up to refill his tea cup. 'And I've said yes. I need something to … keep me busy.'

'And, of course,' Gabriel continued, acting as if he'd known them both all his life, 'I'm so sorry about your father.'

'Thanks,' said Arthur coldly. He grabbed a biscuit and headed for the door. 'I'm off out. Yaz is waiting for me.'

'Don't be back too late!' his mum said. Before Arthur could respond, she had already turned back to her new visitor. 'Now, can I convince you to have a second slice of winberry pie? The winberries are like small blueberries. They grow right up on the Stiperstones, you know.'

'I do, as a matter of fact,' said Gabriel. 'And your cooking is a true marvel!'

Arthur slammed the door. Outside at the front of the cottage, he had to pick his way through piles of rubble. Most of their old chimney had been demolished and was being re-built, so the usually tidy garden was a tip. Arthur kicked a few stones in fury. *Who the hell does this bloke think he is? How dare he talk like that … Ow! What was that?*

Down by his feet, something glinted in the sunlight. *What was it with builders*, he thought, *leaving their rubbish everywhere?* He knelt down to take a closer look.

'Digging for treasure, are we?' said Yaz, peering over the wall.

Arthur jumped. 'Glad you're feeling well enough to creep up on me.' He turned back and used his fingers to dig round the half-buried object. 'And in answer to your question, yes I am!' He tugged hard and held up what looked like a lump of curly leather held together by some kind of big metal clasp.

'What is it?' asked Yaz.

Arthur rubbed the clasp against his jeans. 'I think it's a shoe. A very old one by the look of it.'

'Looks more like a lump of old dog turd to me!'

'Thanks, Yaz. Really helpful. Anyway, since when did dogs start crapping silver buckles? I think my grandma told me about this. It was a custom when they built houses in the old days. They used to brick up a child's shoe in the chimney.'

'What was the point of that?'

'Luck. And also to ward off evil spirits.'

They both fell silent, thinking about last night.

'Let's have a look then,' said Yaz.

'Stick it in your bag. We'll check it out later.' He handed over the shoe and Yaz frowned.

'Do I have to? It's dirty. And I'll have you know this bag is designer!' Yaz put the offending lump into a side pocket.

'Right. And our village is now a fashion catwalk,' Arthur replied.

'*Cat*walk might be the wrong word to use.' Yaz winced. She felt the strange dizziness again, though it quickly passed.

Arthur didn't notice. 'Anyway, can we get out of here?' He looked angrily back through the kitchen window. He could just see his mother smiling at *that man*. It just didn't look right.

Yaz studied the smart, black Mercedes parked outside. 'She hasn't already got a new boyfriend, has she?'

Arthur's face went red. 'Yaz,' he said, clenching his fists, 'you're a good mate. But you've got a big gob. Shut it.'

She looked down. 'Sorry. You're right. Yeah, me and my big mouth. But him –' she pointed at the car – 'all the village is talking about him. He's well posh, from down south somewhere. Made his money in aeroplanes. Did you see his son at school today? Weird eyes. What's he doing round at yours?'

They walked on down the lane towards the village.

'I don't know,' replied Arthur. 'He says he's away a lot. Says he wants paid help round the house. Weird thing is that when I met him, I had this question in my mind. And then it was like he answered it without me speaking …'

'Right. So, talking cats last night and today a mind-reading stranger. I don't think it's me who needs the doctor!'

Arthur shook his head. 'My mum went all smiley around him, as if he was some Hollywood star. I felt like I didn't know her.'

'Well, Diana down at the village shop said he was dead good-looking.'

'Doesn't matter what he looks like. How can she smile when Dad's missing?'

At the end of the lane, the road forked into the hills. On the bend, two stone pillars reared up, topped by carved stone angels. The iron gate between them was rusted. The yew hedges on either side were overgrown. Through the gates, up a long gravel drive, they could just make out Fall Hall. The great stone building had lain empty for years. Its vast windows were shuttered and walls filled with cracks. No one had known who it belonged to, until now.

'Bit big for the two of them,' said Yaz. 'No wonder he needs some help.'

Arthur had that strange feeling again. The house was staring at him. It didn't need a keep out sign to say that they weren't welcome.

As they turned away and headed into the village towards Yaz's house, they heard a sudden ear-splitting screech from above.

They both looked up to see the sun blotted out by a pair of wings. A second screech echoed round the buildings as the wings pulled in and the huge bird dropped straight towards them.

Arthur and Yaz stood, staring up like a pair of dummies, as sharp talons descended, ready for impact.

CHAPTER 5

Arthur could see the cruel beak, curled like an old-fashioned scythe, and just as sharp. And it was closing in – fast.

They both put up their hands to shield their heads. But at the very last moment, instead of the tearing of talons, all they felt was a whoosh of air. The bird hovered briefly right in front of their faces, then flew straight up again.

'That was close!' said Yaz.

'Close? Birdy there could have ripped our faces off!'

'You've been watching too many horror movies. It was a buzzard and, as far as I know, the biggest thing a buzzard will rip into is a rabbit, not a full-size human.'

'Yeah right, Yaz. Just stop being so smug for a moment. As far as you *knew*, big cats were a bunch of old wives' tales too!' Arthur felt shaken. His whole world had changed in the last month. The local wildlife going psycho did not help.

'Point taken,' said Yaz.

'And what did bonkers birdy want with us?'

'Nothing. Maybe we were just standing in the way. But it looked like he dropped something.'

'What? Bird droppings? On our heads? Just what we need … oh …'

Arthur watched as Yaz bent down and picked something out of the overgrown grass at the side of the lane. She held it up towards him.

'Oh!' said Arthur again. He could feel tears stinging his eyes. He took a deep breath, squeezed his eyes shut, then opened them. Yaz handed him a gold ring with a square-cut green stone in the middle.

'It's his, isn't it?' Yaz said. 'I remember seeing him wear it.'

Arthur also remembered the last time he'd gone swimming with his dad, in the River Onny. There was a great spot to jump in where the river curled in a lazy loop. It had been the perfect May day: bright blue dragonflies hovering and shoals of tiny fish in the shallows, darting like magnetic iron filings. His father's ring glinted in the sunlight as he dared Arthur to dive-bomb. The cold water had given him a perfect shock to the skin as he'd landed.

'He's dead,' said Arthur. 'He must be. This proves it.' He imagined the washed-up corpse and the buzzard pecking away at the bloated finger, before finally ripping the joint from its socket to grab at the gold.

But Yaz shook her head. 'No. You've got it totally wrong. This is a message. Your dad's alive; I can feel it.'

Arthur stuffed the ring in his pocket. How dare she try to raise his hopes? He turned and stomped off down the lane.

'No, wait up, Artie.' Yaz came up behind him. 'Think about all the things that have happened since last night.

I know it seems weird, but why would some wild bird fly down and deliver your own father's ring to you? How did it know you're his son? Answer me that?'

Arthur couldn't. 'I dunno,' he growled. 'Nothing makes any sense.'

'OK. Let's drop it for now. Come back to mine. Mum's making samosas.'

Arthur sighed. 'Yeah, sure. Whatever. I never say no to food.'

Yaz's house was a few minutes out of the village, almost hidden in its own small valley. The tiny cottage was built of stone. Small leaded windows shone like diamonds in the afternoon sun.

It was cool inside, the cold stone floor keeping out the summer heat.

'Good to see you, Arthur!' Yaz's mother was as short as her daughter, with the same black hair, tied back. 'Though if you do go off into the wilds again with my daughter, please take a tin of cat food!'

'Ha ha,' said Yaz. It seemed that everyone believed the doctor's story.

Mrs Mitchell lifted a wooden spoon to her lips. 'Not bad! If I say so myself.'

Arthur sniffed, his nose filling with enticing smells. 'I always love your food, Tahira,' he said, grinning.

Mrs Mitchell beamed. 'And who says teenagers only grunt these days? With compliments like that, you are welcome to move in any time. Mind you, Yaz made the dhal. You'll have to see if it's up to scratch!'

Half an hour later, Arthur was eyeing the last samosa on the plate.

'What do you think?' said Yaz.

'Perfect, except for the dhal ...' He could see Yaz narrow her eyes at him. 'Only joking! Brilliant. Fantastic. Beats the takeaway in town.'

Yaz smiled.

'Of course it does,' said Mrs Mitchell. 'Canned vegetables with powdered spices are an insult!'

Arthur wasn't really listening. 'Can I have the last one, please?'

'Go ahead. In fact, I won't forgive you if you leave it on the plate!' Mrs Mitchell looked fondly at the boy. He'd lost so much. What he needed, she thought, what everyone needed, was to know for certain what had happened to his father. It was a shocking thing for the whole village.

Yaz's sister was out playing so they had their shared bedroom to themselves. Yaz had taken a knife and a baking tray from the kitchen. The old shoe Arthur found lay curled up in the middle of the tray.

'I still don't get why we're doing this?' Yaz had already managed to cut away most of the dried-up clay from the outside of the shoe.

'Because we've got nothing better to do,' said Arthur. 'Here. Let me have a go.' He took the knife and stabbed it into the clay that filled the space where a foot once fitted. 'Urghhh!' he grunted. 'Hold the toe bit and I'll try to lever this out!'

Yaz grabbed both ends of the shoe and Arthur pushed against the knife. With a sudden jerking motion, a clod flew up and smashed against the ceiling, showering them with dust.

'Oh, great!' said Yaz. 'Mum will kill me now.'

'Shhh!' said Arthur. 'I can see something!'

'What? More mud? Yes, I can see it now. The discovery of the century. Real hundred-year-old mud with actual dead worms. Must be worth a fortune.'

Arthur ignored her. He pushed his forefinger and thumb deep into the shoe. Then, like a magician pulling a rabbit from a hat, he pulled out what looked like slip of rolled-up, crushed, waxy paper.

'OK. I take it back!' said Yaz. 'Now, if that's a treasure map, I want fifty per cent.'

'We'll see. Can you turn your desk light on?'

Yaz flipped the switch and Arthur carefully unrolled the tattered paper under the light. It was a small, stained square, with cracks that were nearly tearing it apart from where it had been tightly squashed. Tiny writing scrawled across its surface. And, though the letters curved all over the place, the words were clear as Arthur slowly began to read:

Tend to the sleepers else ... the earth shall be shaken apart.

CHAPTER 6

The door to the bedroom slammed open, crashing against the wall. A gust of wind ruffled the paper.

'Ahh! What the …?' Yaz jumped up, wild-eyed.

Arthur didn't move. He stared through the doorway, listening. 'It's OK, Yaz. It's just the breeze. It's not a ghost. Or maybe it's an earthquake,' he said, thinking about Mr Stockheart's lesson.

Yaz stared at the door. 'Sorry. I'm just a bit jumpy. This place is always draughty. Anyway, so much for "X marks the spot". This *Tend to the sleepers* thing sounds like an old saying, the sort of thing my granddad would go on about.'

'What, like "out of the frying pan and into the fire"?'

'Exactly like that.' Yaz walked over to close the door, then sat down by the desk. She rubbed her shoulder. 'Ow. It keeps hurting, you know. I can forget about it, but then I get a bad twinge sometimes.'

Arthur, however, wasn't listening. As he carefully smoothed out the paper again, it gave off a bad smell, like rancid beef fat. 'There's more. Listen.'

'Tis the custom since times gone by to feed the sleepers on the night before midsummer.

Arthur stopped. He had the most weird feeling.
The words sounded like they were already inside his head.
Not only that but they made sense. He blinked a few times
then continued.

*Tend them well with platters of the best that beast
and field have to offer. On this night alone may
they wake, take sustenance and then fall back to
guard that which lays below. She must not wake,
else the dark will be day and the night a landscape
of foul things that move and mew with menace …*

Whatever breeze had blown into the room had now
gone. But despite the warmth outside, they both felt cold.
As far as they could see, nothing had changed. The door
was still shut. The desk was cluttered with homework and
the beds in the corners were just as messy and filled with
shadows. But the air was different, charged, as if it was the
paper that was plugged into the socket, not the lamp.

Arthur couldn't read any more. The words whirled round
in his head. 'My granddad told me about this once,' he said.
'There was a custom that his father used to take part in as
a child. As the sun set on the night before midsummer, the
villagers took a plate of their finest food and laid it at the
mouth of the old lead mine, right under the Stiperstones.
They didn't really know why they were doing it. They just
called it the Festival of Sleep. By midsummer dawn, all the
plates were clean. Everyone thought it was animals who
stole the food. The next day, there was a great big party with
singing and dancing. But as time went on, the whole thing
was banned by the church elders who said it was pagan and
had to stop. No one's been up to the mine now for years.'

'So? Hang on a second, *the night before midsummer*? That's only two nights away,' said Yaz.

'Yeah,' Arthur replied. 'This is going to sound silly – but, maybe that's why we found it now. What if –'

Yaz butted in. 'The writer was talking about *foul things*? Read that bit again!'

Arthur looked down at the paper. '*Foul things that move and mew with menace.*'

They both looked at each other and spoke at the same time. 'The cat!'

Yaz's instinct was to grab the paper and chuck it straight into the nearest fire. But instead she wondered out loud, 'And who is this "She"?'

'Dunno. Listen, there's a bit more.' Arthur tried to keep his voice steady.

Keep the golden arrow safe. It is both key and lock and, in the hands of those with right on their side, it is a burning spear. The golden arrow has been entrusted to our family. The burden is great, but carry it well. Clara Hatfield, the year of our Lord 1872.

By now, Yaz was standing over Arthur, who had turned a pale shade of milk. 'The name?' she asked.

'Yeah. The name. That's my … great-great-grandma. I was always told she was the dotty one.'

'Maybe she was.'

'And maybe she wasn't.' Arthur swallowed hard. The hairs on his arms were prickling. 'My dad had a key-ring in the shape of an arrow. It was all bashed about, not worth anything. He told me it was a family heirloom. Carried it with him everywhere.'

The room was silent. Outside, they could hear Yaz's sister running around, squealing with a friend. The roses were in bloom out the window, and the early evening sun rested on the floorboards in front of them. Life was normal. But this message from the past wasn't normal.

'So these ramblings might mean something ?'

Yaz's question hung in the air.

There was something at the back of Arthur's mind. What was it? He tried to remember. His dad's keys, his clothes, everything he'd left in a neatly folded pile at the side of the quarry pool. What had happened to it all?

Yaz clicked her fingers in front of Arthur's face. 'Are you OK?'

'What? Yeah. Thinking …'

'And?'

Arthur struggled to pull himself back from the nightmare of memories of that day. 'That arrow key-ring of my dad's. It's down at the police station with all his stuff until the inquest. I reckon we have to get it.'

Yaz breathed out, suddenly exhausted. 'You know what, Artie? I think yesterday is catching up with me. I don't feel so brilliant. This stuff is all a bit much right now. But if you think it'll do any good, let's go after school tomorrow. Yeah?'

'You're right. I'm done in too.' Arthur stood up to go, folding the paper carefully. 'Thanks for the nosh. It was well tasty.'

Yaz opened the door and they walked downstairs.

'You two all right? Looks like you've seen a ghost!' Mrs Mitchell said as they crossed the kitchen.

'Nah, just tired,' Arthur mumbled. 'Thanks for having me.' And then he was out of the door and heading back home.

The sun was sinking lower towards the hills. Arthur put his hand in his pocket and felt the ring there. He couldn't face taking it out to look at it yet, but he allowed himself one mad thought. Maybe his dad *was* still out there, somewhere. And maybe pigs had wings after all.

As he passed the gates of Fall Hall, he heard a sniggering sound. Arthur turned round.

Jack Mytton stood on the other side of the gates, gripping them with both hands. His pale face squeezed between two iron struts with a smug expression.

'Football … tomorrow afternoon.' The boy's voice was unusually deep and grating, as if he had a permanent cough.

Arthur didn't know how to respond. 'Yeah. It beats PE, I suppose.'

'I play to win, you know.'

Arthur noticed the boy's fingernails needed a good trim. 'Good. I mean great. No point playing to lose is there?'

'None at all, Arthur Hatfield. Be seeing you then.' The green eyes held on to him for a further few seconds. Then the boy loped off up the gravelled drive.

Arthur was puzzled. Though the conversation had been pretty harmless, why did it feel like every word had been a threat?

CHAPTER 7

Tuesday, two days before midsummer

It was two in the afternoon and both teams were doing warm-ups on the pitch. Heavy June clouds filled the sky, threatening thunder with far-off rumbles.

Better than being stuck in a muggy classroom, thought Arthur as he jogged on the spot. Central defender suited him. He was quick on his legs and had a knack for working out when an attack was coming. He turned round and gave the thumbs-up to the goalie.

They were certainly in with a chance as his team, the Myndtowners, represented the best that lower school could offer.

However, despite it only being his second day, Jack Mytton had somehow managed to convince the other team, Wentnor Wanderers, to make him captain. With his kit on, the boy's pale skin appeared to be bleached. As he did a series of star jumps, the girls on the sideline were actually *ooh*ing and making comments about muscles and good looks. It was even more reason to hate him.

The two captains shook hands and a coin was flipped. From the start, the game was half-hearted. The girls quickly lost interest and only cheered when Jack had the ball. There were endless fumbles, passes that failed and the ball itself never moved away from the central part of the pitch. Even the ref seemed distracted. He gave an offside to Wentnor when it was obvious that the Myndtown striker was nowhere near the goal.

Then suddenly the ball was flying through the air straight towards Arthur. He had two choices: play safe and punt it back to the goalie, or give it the big shot as his striker headed up the pitch to an open spot in the other half. He made the right move, belting the ball with his boot, then watching it soar into the sky.

But out of the corner of Arthur's eye, he noticed Jack Mytton. The boy was miles away from the ball. And it wasn't Mytton's job to play defence. But this didn't stop him gliding up the pitch in a blur. Before the Myndtown striker knew what was happening, Mytton had butted in, chesting the ball back on to the ground. In the next moment, he was over the halfway line and sprinting straight towards Arthur. He didn't bother dribbling the ball, which appeared to be super-glued to his feet. Mytton also seemed to forget that he was part of a team as he ignored the shouts for him to pass.

Instead, he forged ahead. And this was where Arthur got confused. The girls were cheering like mad. Even Yaz waved her arms in the air. For a moment, Arthur wondered if Jack Mytton had grown an extra pair of legs. He rubbed his eyes. No normal person ran that fast. But no one else seemed to notice as the distance shrank between them. Before Arthur could even think about it, Mytton had pulled up right in front of him, wearing that same smirk on his face.

'Like I said,' Mytton hissed so that only Arthur could hear, 'I play to win! You might as well give up now, *boy*!'

Arthur held his ground, dancing to the left and right to put off any sudden moves from Mytton. He was aware that the other defenders hadn't even caught up and that Mytton only needed one decent kick to score. He had to get the ball off him. But as he moved forward to block the attack, something slammed into his memory. He'd heard the voice before. Not that long ago. And that was impossible.

Thinking about it cost Arthur any advantage. His team-mates looked on with dismay as their best defender stood there in a daze while Mytton slipped round him. Defenders were supposed to move, not practice being a statue.

Jack Mytton kicked the ball so hard it almost burst. The Myndtown goalie was good. He even managed to dive to the right, the side that the ball shot towards. It should have been a simple save. The goal keeper caught it, but the momentum of the ball carried him backwards. There was a nasty crack as the goalie's head bounced off the post. With a life of its own, the ball slipped out his hands and slammed into the back of the net. The goalie tumbled over, then groggily tried to get to his feet.

There was a second's silence as the audience and both teams tried to comprehend what had just happened. It was a goal, but a goal unlike any they'd seen before.

Then the crowd went wild. No one really cared if it all seemed a bit odd. The Wentnor crew lifted Mytton on to their shoulders and chanted, 'One–nil, one–nil, one–nil!'

Not the most original song in the world, thought Arthur. He felt ashamed of himself. How could he have stood there like that? The game resumed at the same dull pace as before. Within minutes, the clouds finally let rip and gave everyone a good soaking. Both teams soon resembled a pack of mud-monsters. There was plenty of sliding about, but no more goals. In the shower rooms, after the match, Arthur was given the cold shoulder by his team-mates.

'No hard feelings, eh?' Jack smirked, as he passed Arthur in the corridor at the end of the school day.

'No feelings at all,' muttered Arthur.

Jack paused, his green eyes flickering up and down the empty corridor. 'It felt good kicking that ball and watching it shoot like an *arrow* towards the goalie.' He winked at Arthur, then walked off.

'What was that about?' said Yaz as she came up behind Arthur and watched Jack stalk away.

'Nothing,' Arthur grunted.

'He really can move!'

'What is it with you girls? There's more to life than being able to aim a bit of inflated cowhide!'

'Ooh! I do believe that you, young Hatfield, are having a sulk!'

'No,' said Arthur, 'it's more than that. There's something wrong about that boy.'

Yaz twirled a bit of gum round with her fingers. 'Hmm. Plenty wrong. Muscles like mountains, moves like a dancer and black hair to die for. Sounds like a severe infection of jealousy to me. Right, we'd better run if we're going to catch the school bus. Then are we off to the police station?'

Arthur had forgotten about their plan. 'I dunno. What's the point. I bet those stories about my great-great-grandma were spot on. She was nuts!' He felt like he was losing everything: his dad, his confidence, the stupid game. What was the point in anything?

'Arthur. Look at me. Yaz. Your best mate. Now, I am pretty sure we weren't chased off the Stiperstones by a *pet*. And I'm also sure that if the shoe fits, wear it.'

'You mean see where it leads us?'

'I do. Now come on!'

However, an hour later, PC Jones was shooing them out of the door. 'Sorry, guys. That nice Mr Mytton was here not half an hour ago to pick up your dad's stuff.'

'What? He's got no right!' Arthur shouted.

'Calm down, Arthur,' said PC Jones. 'Let me explain. He came in on behalf of your mum. He said she was in a bit of a state and he wanted to help out. I must say it's good to have someone so thoughtful moving into the village.'

'Thoughtful!' Arthur exploded. 'My mum only met the man yesterday and now he's fingering through my dad's personal stuff!'

PC Jones was taken aback. 'Listen, Artie, I know you're going through a lot. He was only trying to be helpful.'

Yaz grabbed hold of his sleeve. 'PC Jones is right. Come on, let's go home.'

Arthur frowned as he was led unwillingly outside. First the son, now the father. It didn't make sense. What kind of game were they playing?

CHAPTER 8

Tuesday, late afternoon

Arthur closed his hand round the ring that was still in his pocket. Even if his dad was dead, *that* man had a nerve. 'We're going to sort this, right now!'

'Artie, think about it!' Yaz was trying to keep up as Arthur strode away from the police station.

'Think about what?'

'Your mum *has* been in a state, which isn't surprising. And so are you. Just because Mr Mytton tried to help out, it doesn't mean he's got some evil plan up his sleeve!'

'I don't give a monkey's about evil plans. He's taken my dad's stuff. I'm going to get it. Are you coming or not?'

'Oh, all right. If only to keep you out of trouble.'

Yaz almost had to jog to keep up, but as they walked Arthur noticed something different about the village.

'Where is everybody?' he wondered.

'What do you mean?' said Yaz.

'Well, Mrs Beddoes is usually out doing her veg plot. And old Tony is always leaning on his gate and chatting to everyone who passes …' The village felt empty. Even his own house had seemed silent when they'd passed it earlier.

He wondered whether his mum had come home from work yet.

Yaz shook her head. 'I dunno. Maybe they've gone to the loo or to make a cup of tea. Hey, I've got it!' She beamed and said, 'They've turned into zombies and are about to rip off your arm and eat it, served with eyeball pie!'

'Helpful,' said Arthur.

'My pleasure,' Yaz replied.

The gates of Fall Hall looked as forbidding as ever. The carved stone angels on top of the pillars stared at them from hollow eye sockets.

'Creepy, just like the movies!' Yaz said, rolling her eyes. 'Now all we need is the gates to creak as we open them!'

However, the hinges had been mended and the gate swung smoothly and silently open. Gravel crunched beneath their feet all the way up the drive. The path was lined with thickets of overgrown shrubs. Purple flowers gave off a thick, cloying scent.

Fall Hall appeared as unfriendly as the last time they had seen it. Though the shutters on some of the windows had been opened, the house squatted in front of them like a fat, grey toad. A sweep of stone steps led up to the massive black door, with a knocker in the shape of an angel's head.

'You first,' said Yaz.

Arthur wasn't so sure. Now that they were here, his legs felt like turning right round and making a run for it. *Ridiculous! He had every right!* As he hesitated, they both heard the sound of singing coming from somewhere inside.

Whatever song it was, the effect was instant. It reminded Arthur of the last Christmas service he'd been to. The local choir had sung something that had been written over six hundred years ago. Arthur had lost interest the moment the choirmaster had begun talking. But when the choir started he had felt like he was hearing hundreds of voices from the past. And now this song felt similar, though it was only one mournful voice. The sad melody seeped through the old stone of Fall Hall.

Arthur and Yaz were both mesmerized. It was like the Pied Piper. They had no choice but to follow the rise and fall of the song round the edge of the house, skirting the crumbling remains of an old walled garden.

As they crept closer to the source of the sound, the sadness of the music took over. Yaz found herself thinking of her old cat Merlin and how, when he was finally too frail to move, it was she who had held and stroked him as the vet gave the injection that sent him to sleep forever.

Arthur thought of his dad, felt the ache in his heart for every awful joke he'd ever told. He remembered every stone they'd skimmed together on the local rivers. Now his father was gone, and this strange song brought it all back again. He couldn't even fight the tears and he wasn't aware that his face was soaking wet as he pressed his nose against a window.

They had reached a corner at the back of the house. The gloomy ground-floor window had been cleaned recently, though cobwebs still clung to the inner edges. Yaz slumped down against the wall while Arthur peered in.

It took him a few moments to adjust to the light before he saw that it was a bedroom. A huge wardrobe in the corner had doors that hung open. In the middle of the room, a double bed was strewn with clothes. A tall figure stood within, with his back to the window.

The song died and the figure remained absolutely still. The man was wearing a pair of smart black trousers but was bare from the waist up.

Arthur's nose was blocked from crying. He wanted to blow it or sniff but knew that it wasn't a good idea. The moment the song stopped, the memories of his father vanished. He felt gutted, as if his dad was just out of reach round the corner.

The man turned towards the wardrobe. As he did, Arthur saw that his back seemed strange. It wasn't twisted or anything like that. But where the shoulder blades should have been, there were two bright red bony nubs. The skin was inflamed and the nubs were sharp, like a pair of tiny mountains. The effect was disturbing.

Arthur ducked down and turned to Yaz. 'Check this out!' he whispered. But Yaz was still lost in her own thoughts. Arthur swivelled back and stared into the room.

The figure stood there, perfectly still, now facing him directly. Arthur recognized the clear, blue eyes that gazed into his. And those eyes saw everything. All of Arthur's hurt was laid bare, every ache in his heart flipped open like a book. Arthur could also see the sadness in the man's eyes. It was endless, beyond tears, beyond time.

Arthur blinked.

There was the bed. There was the wardrobe. But the room was empty. In the brief moment between his eyelids opening and closing, the man had vanished.

CHAPTER 9

'How are you, Arthur?' Gabriel Mytton was standing right behind them outside the window, wearing a white shirt, open at the neck.

Arthur's heart missed a beat. 'I'm … fine. How did you …?' He couldn't think of the words to say. 'But you were inside and now you're …'

'Outside. Yes. Legs are amazing things, really,' said Gabriel. 'They can walk to a door, open it, take this poor old body to the back of a house and round the side. So here we are. And here you are, looking through my window.'

It seemed like a perfectly reasonable explanation.

No way, thought Arthur. Just one second ago, the man was inside the room staring at him. He couldn't be in two places at once. So how had he crept up on them?

Gabriel did up the top button of his shirt. 'Do please introduce me to your friend.'

'I … errr, this is Yaz. Yasmeen. This is Mr Mytton.'

'Oh, please, call me Gabriel.'

Arthur wondered why Yaz didn't appear at all surprised. But then he remembered she hadn't seen what he had.

'Nice to meet you.' Yaz stared in fascination at the man's eyes. All thoughts of her cat vanished. Instead, all she could think about was how his eyes were the exact same shade of blue used by painters in the old days to create the skies behind angels.

'Now that you've both arrived, I think that tea's ready. Do join me,' Gabriel insisted, as though he had been waiting for them. As he led them round towards the front of the house, he put his arm on Arthur's shoulder as though they were old friends. The man's hand felt lighter than a feather.

'I suffered a terrible flying accident some years ago,' he continued as they reached the front steps. 'I was lucky to get out alive. But my back still bears the scars. They keep me awake at night.'

Arthur knew that Gabriel was deliberately telling him something about the weird lumps on his shoulders.

'Poor you,' said Yaz.

'Yes, poor me!' agreed Gabriel, his words pouring like honey. 'Now, please, come inside.'

They climbed the lichen-covered steps. One of the huge doors swung open, held by a sulky looking Jack.

'There you are, my boy. Now, off to the kitchen with you.' Gabriel smiled, but his tone was sharp.

Jack slunk away. 'I'm no one's *boy*!' he muttered under his breath.

Arthur and Yaz's first vision of Fall Hall was a gloomy entrance hall that led to a long, shadowy corridor lined with antlers and stuffed animal heads to the left and right.

'Yes, my ancestors were somewhat barbaric,' said Gabriel, answering Arthur's thoughts. 'It was shoot first, ask questions later!' The stone floor echoed with their footsteps. They passed many sets of double doors, each of which had the stuffed head of a giant cat above it. Glass eyes glittered and jaws were frozen in mid-bite, revealing teeth that caused Yaz to shudder.

'Of course,' Gabriel continued, 'there were no tigers in Shropshire. But the Myttons happily travelled the Empire, doing their bit to speed up the extinction of certain species. I'm rather ashamed of them. It's important to respect savage creatures, don't you think?'

He paused under the head of a white tiger and pushed open the doors.

A huge rectangle of a room was revealed before them. One wall was lined with books that climbed up to the ceiling, way above their heads. The far wall revealed large shuttered windows that looked out to what had once been a lawn at the back of the house. Nature had taken over; now it was a wilderness, doing its best to creep up through the glass.

'As you can see, there's a lot of work to get done. Do take a seat,' said Gabriel.

There were old, threadbare sofas spread about the room and a scattering of chairs. Even though it was summer, the room felt cold and damp.

'Yes. We need warming up and …' Gabriel paused and cocked his head to one side. 'I do believe that the solution is here!'

Another door opened and in came Arthur's mother, bearing a tray with a pot of tea and china cups.

Arthur jumped up. 'Mum, what are you doing here?'

'Oh, don't mind me,' she said, putting the tray down. 'And there was I thinking that working at the café was good. This place is a treasure trove. And you should see the size of the kitchen – we could fit our whole house inside it, Artie! It's very good of Mr Mytton to give me the work, now that ...' Her face crumpled.

'There, there, Christina. Not good to dwell on the past, hmmm?' The moment Gabriel spoke, she smiled, as though a switch had been flicked on.

It was as they were sipping their tea and tucking into chocolate brownies straight from the oven that Arthur forced himself to remember why they had come. He put his cup down and stared at Gabriel. 'You took my father's stuff.'

'Yes,' Gabriel admitted. 'It was the least I could do. Your poor mother. The last month has been such a strain for you both.'

Gabriel's niceness was a fog that Arthur had to fight his way through. Everything he said seemed to be so reasonable. Arthur almost nodded in agreement, but he was not going to be put off. 'Well, I'd like my dad's key-ring back. There was an old family thing on there, made of gold metal, worthless really ...'

'You mean the *arrow*?' The blue eyes rested on him.

'Yeah,' said Arthur, 'I do.' His anger returned. Who did this guy think he was?

His mother broke the silence. 'Oh, that old thing? Why would you want that, Artie? Gabriel is doing some research on local history. Look!' She swung her arm round to show the wall of books. 'He thinks the arrow might be part of an ancient local custom. He'd like to spend some time working on it, wouldn't you, Gabe?'

Gabriel sat back in his armchair, pressing his fingers into a steeple shape as he nodded.

Mrs Hatfield carried on. 'Well, I said, it's no good to me, so I thought to myself, he might as well have it …'

Arthur looked at his mother. He knew she liked to rabbit on, but this was weird. She was talking and talking while Gabriel looked on as if she was some kind of animal performing an interesting trick.

'Exactly so, my dear Tina. Now if you don't mind, Arthur, I'd like to hold on to it for a little while longer. Well, at least until midsummer dawn is over.'

The last words felt like they were for Arthur alone. He looked round. Neither Yaz nor his mother seemed to have noticed what he'd said.

And suddenly there it was, held between the man's forefinger and thumb. It was no bigger than a matchstick, with a bent shaft and dull point. A *golden arrow*? It was more like a rusty pin.

As Gabriel gripped the tiny arrow, his voice grew both softer and stronger. 'It's time for both of you to be leaving, I think.'

Like a puppet, Yaz stood up. 'As Gabriel says, time for us to go.' She turned to Arthur's mother. 'Serious brownies, Mrs H.'

Mrs Hatfield gave a pretend curtsey.

Arthur couldn't take his eyes off the arrow. What had Clara Hatfield said? *It was both lock and key* ... and something about a *weapon*. A weapon that was now pointed directly at him.

'Goodbye, Arthur. Time really is running out, and we wouldn't want your mother returning in the dark, would we?'

CHAPTER 10

Tuesday night

Yaz woke up in a panic. Her forehead was drenched with sweat. What was that sound? The window was open, curtains flapping in the breeze. She heard her sister snuffling in her sleep.

There! Again! Scratching at the window. She wanted to shrink into her bed. The cat had come for her! She knew it. It wanted to finish her off this time. Underneath the bandages, her shoulder felt worse than ever. It was swollen and hot. The brave thing to do would be to run to the window and slam it shut before the beast could get in. But Yaz was fixed to her bed, her eyes staring and waiting.

'Yaz!'

She heard the whisper rise through the window. Oh no! Arthur was right. It *was* a talking cat after all!

But then her thoughts cleared. Unless the cat was also a great mimic, she could stop worrying.

She forced herself to breathe slowly and eased herself from under the duvet. Stepping over to the window, she quietly pulled the curtains apart to reveal a broom rubbing against one of the panes. She almost smiled. At least the broom didn't have a witch riding it. Yaz pushed the window open wider and leaned out.

'What do you want?' she whispered.

Arthur was standing in the garden, holding the broom above his head. 'We need to go, now!' he hissed.

'Go where? Artie, it's the middle of the night. I was just having a lovely nightmare!'

'And that man weaving his weird spells on my mum is a *real* nightmare! We have to get the arrow. For my dad's sake.'

Just for a moment, he allowed himself to hope again. Maybe the arrow would lead him to his father. Alive or dead. Maybe … And Gabriel Mytton had talked about time running out and midsummer dawn, which was only a day and a half away. Arthur felt a pressure in his heart pushing him onwards.

Yaz groaned. 'How?'

'Come down. Time for a moonlit walk!'

'Do I have to?'

'No. Go back to sleep if you want. I'll go by myself.' Arthur crossed his arms and looked down.

'Oh no! I can't stand it when you sulk,' she whispered. 'OK. Give me time to get changed.'

Five minutes later, the side door slowly swung open.

'This is mad!' Yaz muttered. 'Mum and Dad will kill us if they find out'.

Arthur didn't reply, setting off down the lane towards the village. The moon was growing fuller each night and the hills were gilded with silver.

Yaz ran after him, looking back nervously at the cottage. 'I don't want to think what will happen if I'm found missing from my bed.'

They walked on in silence until they were standing by a crumbling stone wall that lined the lane to Fall Hall.

'Up and over you go!' said Arthur.

'Why can't we use the gate?' Yaz hissed.

'Because, if we're going to break and enter, walking in the front might not be so brilliant!'

'What if he's got attack dogs?' Yaz asked as she found a foothold and heaved herself up.

'Then we'll be a right dog's dinner.'

Yaz gasped and looked down at him. 'Thanks!'

'You're welcome. Here, take my bag,' Arthur pulled off his rucksack and handed it up. It was heavy.

'*Oof*. What have you got in here?'

'A couple of tins of cat food,' said Arthur, 'and some other magic ingredients.'

'Why? Are we on a pet-rescue mission?'

'I wish! I'll explain later.' He tapped his nose and climbed up.

Together they both balanced on top of the wall, which wound its way along the lane like a twisted snake. The view into the estate was hidden by bushes. A shrill cry from a nearby tree startled them. Yaz nearly lost her footing and she grabbed hold of Arthur to stop herself falling.

'That's it!' she hissed. 'I'm out of here!'

'Just an owl,' Arthur replied. 'You do know that we live in the countryside? And,' he added, 'it's not the owls we should be afraid of.'

Yaz frowned. 'Yeah, right. Thanks so much for the helpful words. Still, I suppose we've come this far. Go on. You first this time.'

Once they were over the wall, they made their way through a thicket of sharp bushes until they reached the edge of the lawn.

'This can't be right,' Arthur muttered. 'Look! Where did all the weeds go?' In the space of a few hours, the waist-high jungle had vanished. Now, there was a perfectly smooth, grassy lawn leading to the library at the back of Fall Hall. Box hedges, pruned into the shapes of various animals dotted the lawn. They looked like living statues.

From their hiding place under the last bush, Yaz reached out a hand. The grass was dewy and soft as hair. 'Lawnmower?' she suggested. 'Army of hedge clippers?'

Then Arthur was off, striding over the strange, perfect lawn, his long shadow thrown backwards.

'You're crazy,' she whispered. 'If anyone happens to look out from the house, you'll be seen.' But Arthur didn't turn round.

Taking a deep breath, Yaz crept across the wide expanse, peering up at the dark windows. The empty blackness gave nothing back. The house simply stood still, the mass of silent stone waiting for them.

Finally, they crouched by one of the library windows. Yaz tapped Arthur's shoulder. 'I really don't think this is such a good idea!'

'Shhhhh!' Using his fingertips, Arthur prised the edges of the window frame. So far, luck had been with them and still their luck held: the catch on the sash window was undone. But as Arthur strained his arms to slide the window up, the old frame protested. The pulleys that raised and lowered the window had not been oiled in a hundred years. They were rusty and the screech they gave out was loud enough to wake the dead.

Arthur and Yaz ducked down, their hearts hammering. A few seconds later, through the open window, they heard the creak of the library door and then a padding sound. This was followed by a deep, ominous rumble. The padding stopped. There was silence.

They scrunched up tighter under the window sill, trying not to breathe. Nothing happened. The silence lengthened. Arthur leaned over and whispered into Yaz's ear. 'Maybe it's gone. I'll have a peek.'

No! Yaz mouthed back.

Arthur ignored her and inched his way up, trying to move as slowly as possible.

The sight that greeted him as he peered in shouldn't have been a surprise. He'd already worked it out. He was even prepared. Or so he thought. But as his eyes pierced the darker shadows of the library, the shape that prowled its length and breadth was unmistakable. A long tail swished back and forth like a whip. It stopped to sniff the air, huge paws resting on the wooden floor.

Big, black cat. Big trouble.

CHAPTER 11

Arthur froze, framed in the window by moonlight. He might as well have painted a target on his head. It would only take a single leap and the cat would be on him. This time, it would not pause before sinking its teeth in.

But Arthur held his ground. There was no breeze and therefore his own human smell would not waft into the room. As long as he stayed silent, he might be in with a chance.

The cat stood there like a suspicious hunter. Arthur felt the power in its taut muscles. It sniffed the air once more. The room was empty. It lowered its head and continued pacing, ignoring the open window.

In slow motion, Arthur bent his knees and sank back down without a sound. He carefully eased opened his rucksack and pulled out the two tins of cat food. Their metal edges glinted under the moonlight.

Wait, he mouthed to Yaz, handing her one of the tins.

They stayed still until, finally, the sound of padding paws grew distant. Further off they heard a door squeak open, then slam shut. The creature was gone.

'Was that what I thought it was?' Yaz whispered.

'I'm afraid so. That's why I brought the tins.'

Yaz was confused. 'But what's it doing here in the house? It's wild!'

'More than wild. Think about it, Yaz. Who else lives here? Same green eyes. Same black hair …'

'But that *thing* tried to rip my back apart the other night. And now you're saying it's … No way!'

'Yes.'

It was too much for Yaz to take in. 'You think it won't kill us because you plan to offer it a few mouthfuls of Mew-Chew?'

'Exactly. Follow me!' Arthur wriggled like a snake through the open window before dropping quietly on to the floor of the library.

Yaz didn't move. Everything Arthur said began to make some sort of sense. Therefore, common sense, plus the pain in her shoulder, told her to run. But her best friend was now inside. With a deep breath, she made up her mind and reluctantly clambered up and over the window sill. By night, the library had changed. Shadows lurked in the corners. Even the chairs looked as though they were about to come to life and attack them. She looked at the tin in her hand and shrugged. 'Not much of a weapon, is it?' she whispered.

Soon they were out in the corridor, using the moonlight that leaked through a small window at the top of the end wall to guide them. There were no sounds except for the tiny squeak of their trainers on the flagstone floor. It was as though the stone walls were holding their breath.

Arthur paused in the middle of the corridor. 'This is the perfect spot!' he whispered. He sat down and pulled the ring on the tin. 'Open your one.' Arthur dug a spoon from his pocket and a small cardboard packet. He scooped out the food and made a tidy mound of it on one of the worn flagstones. Yaz added the contents of her tin.

'Now for the magic ingredient!' Arthur quietly opened the packet.

'Pills?' Yaz whispered.

'Sleeping pills. My mum stopped taking them recently. Best not to have them in the house.' He crushed the pills and mixed them into the smelly mush. 'This is proper recycling.'

'And you don't think Mr Monster Cat will be a tiny bit suspicious?'

'Nah. Animal instincts – never say no to a free nosh.'

'I wish I had your faith. Feels more like going from bad to worse to me. We've just broken in here, found the place guarded by a black-furred beast, who, by the way, may or may not be a football-mad boy by day. Oh, and to top it all, you think you can defeat the bloodthirsty beast with some bits of minced-up dead cow. Please tell me I'm dreaming.' She shook her head in dismay.

'Sorry, Yaz. I know it's weird, but it's no dream. Now then, next problem: where to find the arrow. This place is enormous; it could be anywhere. Where would Gabriel hide it?'

Arthur closed his eyes and thought. As he did, Clara Hatfield's words came back to him. If his family really were like guardians and the arrow belonged to them, then maybe it could be a compass to guide them. He found himself picturing the bent sliver of gold on his dad's key-ring. Immediately, his eyes flew open and were drawn to the far end of the corridor on the right. 'OK,' Arthur breathed. 'Instinct here we come.'

It was one door among many, but as they approached it, they could hear light snoring coming from the other side. It made sense. It had to be the room that they'd both stood outside earlier that day.

'This is it!' Arthur whispered. But suddenly, now he'd got this far, he couldn't go any further. The door might have been made of rock. It didn't need an alarm on it. Every part of it – from the wood panels to the frame and the dark line of shadow under the bottom – said, *Leave now, while you still have the chance.*

Arthur gave in to the feeling. 'Maybe we should just go home,' he said quietly.

But now it was Yaz's turn to act bravely. 'You must be joking. Not when we've come this far. Anyway, that cat is still somewhere behind us so we can't turn around now.' She reached out to touch the brass door handle. It was cold, so cold that her hand seemed to stick to it and it made her fingers tingle. She stopped and stood quite still. Then she shook herself and very gently squeezed and turned. There was a soft click and the door creaked open.

The breathing inside the room changed. Silence. Even now, thought Arthur, Gabriel was probably standing on the other side, waiting for them. He gripped Yaz's arm in terror.

This time, they wouldn't be offered a cup of tea. Arthur's heart was beating like a speed-up drum machine.

There was a sound of sheets shifting, then a long sigh followed by snoring. Arthur and Yaz looked at each other, then they both edged forward, pushing the door a few centimetres at a time until they stood on the threshold. The room was exactly the same as earlier in the day, the large wardrobe dark and looming. However, now the bed was occupied by a curled-up lump – Gabriel.

The pale face was turned towards the door and the long fingers of one hand curled round the pillow. The pillow! Arthur closed his eyes and knew with absolute certainty that the arrow was tucked underneath. It was so obvious it was silly, but he knew that was where he'd find it. All he had to do was take two steps, slide his hand under the pillow and the arrow would be his. As though sleepwalking, he moved forward and his feet sank softly into the carpet. He crept closer, trying not to breathe. Gabriel's face in front of him appeared oddly beautiful. There was not a single wrinkle and the skin was as smooth as bone-china.

Arthur slowly reached towards the pillow, expecting those clear eyes to snap open and Gabriel's hand to shoot out and grab him. His fingers trembled as he eased them under the pillow. Then, with a jolt, his fingertips touched metal. The cool feel of the arrow calmed him down. What was there to worry about? The still-sleeping figure of Gabriel agreed. Nothing happened. The pale face was almost angelic, resting in slumber as Arthur gently eased out the arrow.

He stepped back across the room, glancing down at his feet and nearly gasped out loud. That was why the carpet felt so soft: the floor was covered in grey feathers! His footsteps had been drowned in softness. It was just one more strange thing in a strange night.

More importantly he'd got what he'd came for. Yaz watched nervously as he reached the door. They gave one last glance at Gabriel. Perhaps it was a trick of the moonlight, but the figure in the bed appeared to be glowing. Only instead of light, darkness seemed to pour like a river from Gabriel's breath, filling the room. They had to close the door before the darkness swallowed them!

With a soft click of the latch, Yaz leaned back against the door frame. 'We did it. We're safe!' she whispered.

'Hmm … I don't know about that.' Arthur pointed along the corridor. Underneath the stuffed heads of long-dead lions, tigers and panthers, a living creature had finally caught their scent. This creature did not have glass eyes. Nor was it mounted on a wall. The saliva that dripped from its teeth conveyed only one message, loud and clear.

There was no way out, no bicycles waiting round a corner. The cat gave a satisfied growl.

They'd got away before. Not this time.

CHAPTER 12

'Give it back!' The voice was low and scratchy.

Yaz looked round. 'Who said that?'

'I told you it could speak!' Arthur hissed. 'You didn't believe me!'

'Yeah,' said Yaz, backing away down the corridor. 'Well, it's not every day you meet a chatty pussycat!'

'Talking about it won't save us!' said Arthur, also stepping backwards.

'And your failed stunt with the cat food will?'

They were both trapped and they knew it.

The cat paced slowly towards them, taking its time. It was now only metres away. 'Give it back and I ... promise that your deaths will be quick.'

'Well, that's a relief!' Yaz replied, putting on a show of bravery. 'I'm always up for a short death, me.' She turned to Arthur. 'Please, just do as Claw-Features says.'

But Arthur was stubborn. He faced the beast head on. 'No. Come and get it, you flea-bitten lump of fur!'

'Are you stupid, Artie?' Yaz whispered, an edge of panic in her voice.

The cat paused and lifted one of its massive paws to it's mouth. A giant tongue flicked out, licking round the sharp claws, cleaning them ready for action. 'You would … goad me, boy!'

It couldn't really get any worse, Arthur thought, in which case, there wasn't much to lose. Besides, he wanted some answers and knew he had to keep the beast talking. 'Why is the arrow so important?'

'Why?' the cat grated. 'Why? That arrow has been our jailer. It burned my mistress. Oh, *She* was wailing in such pain. But not for much longer now.'

Yaz stopped looking around for another exit. 'Your mistress? Who is she?'

'Ah, *She* is the mother of all shadows. And this *key* –' the cat spat it out like a swear word – 'this key bound Her tight in a cocoon of sleep. I was Her most faithful servant and would have stayed with Her through all of time.'

Arthur and Yaz were astounded to see green eyes glaze over. Tears trickled down the cat's black face.

The cat continued with a self-pitying mew. 'But no! *She* commanded me, her true familiar, "*Go!*" Slippery like an eel I was. Small as a dancing flea. The spell could not hold *me* who can change form as you humans blink your eyelids. And so I left Her … and prowled these hills, searching through the centuries … for the key to free Her! By midsummer dawn it shall aaall beeee … ovvverrrr.' The cat's speech began to slow down. It stumbled through the last words, slurring them as though it were drunk.

'Are you all right?' said Arthur mockingly. 'You don't sound very well. Are you suffering from indigestion? Perhaps we could call the vet out.'

'Enough!' the cat hissed. Green eyes flashed as it raised itself up with an effort. It leapt straight towards them, one paw raised to strip the skin off their faces.

Yaz flung up her arms and braced herself for impact.

But mid-air, the cat went limp. There was a gigantic thump and the walls shook as the cat landed in a heap on the floor.

'What … what happened?' Yaz asked, shaking all over.

'I … I … I … kept it talking for long enough for the pills to take effect.'

A rumbling snore confirmed the truth and Arthur's legs folded under him and he slid to the floor with his head in his hands. 'I'm sorry, Yaz. That wasn't clever. I'm so stupid. I put us in danger. We should never have come here.'

'Well, that cat food thing was brilliant,' Yaz admitted. 'And we're both stupid because we're still here and guess what?' She grabbed Arthur and yanked him upright. 'If I was asleep in my house and I heard voices and a massive noise, what would I do?'

Arthur groaned.

'Exactly. I'd wake up!' She pointed back the way they'd come. A shaft of light spilled from under the bedroom door. Let's –'

'Go!' Arthur finished.

They ran past Gabriel's bedroom and the cat to the library, just managing to close the door behind them when they heard rapid footsteps and a cry of pain.

A voice called out, clear as rain. 'What have they done to you? Who did this?'

They didn't wait to hear more. They both dived headfirst through the half-open window. Arthur felt gravel dig into his palm and the breath was knocked from his lungs. Yaz's reactions were faster; she forward-rolled her way back to standing.

'Awesome!' Arthur panted, staggering upright.

Yaz swung back to face the house, grabbed the window and pulled it shut. This time, luck held. The frame slid straight down without a screech. They stood and looked across the moonlit lawn. It was in completely plain view.

'Any ideas?' Yaz whispered.

'Leg it!' suggested Arthur. They had no choice but to risk it.

They were halfway across the lawn when a sound stopped them dead in their tracks. Arthur clutched the arrow in his pocket as Gabriel Mytton strode briskly round the side of the house, straight towards them. Arthur grabbed Yaz's hand; better they face it together. They stood stock still. What explanation could they possibly have? Not that it mattered. Anyway, they were two against one. Forget fear. Bring it on, thought Arthur.

But the moon had a strange effect. Arthur felt as though he and Yaz were suddenly just like the bushes on the lawn carved into animal shapes. Somehow, as the grey beams washed over them, he felt frozen in time and couldn't move.

Yaz could barely even turn her eyes to watch as Gabriel advanced. However, as she stared, something dawned on her. The moon was shining so brightly Gabriel should have had have a shadow trailing behind him. He didn't. There was only the emptiness of the grass. It felt horrible. Wrong. She tried to shudder, but her lungs were turned to stone. And the scratches on her shoulder felt worse than ever.

The lack of a shadow was the least of their worries. Gabriel Mytton didn't have claws. He had something far worse. Each set of long, thin fingers held something shiny. Shiny and sharp. Two hands. Two knives. One for each of them.

CHAPTER 13

Gabriel approached them, his hands cradling the lethal blades. Each shiny surface caught the moon. They were honed, ready for cutting.

'Who made my beloved boy ill? Who crept like a fox into my house and stole my arrow?' The words floated on the breeze so softly that Arthur and Yaz could hardly hear them.

They had broken the rules and now they were about to pay. Arthur felt the tiny arrow digging into his palm. His head told him to run, but the arrow asked him to be still. He thought about the drama games they did at school. While the rest of the class managed to hold their breath and strike a pose, Arthur was always the statue that fidgeted. His teacher despaired of his ever getting it right. Anyway, what was the point in standing there like lemons on legs? He felt a twitch in his nose and was desperate to scratch it.

Gabriel Mytton was getting closer now, his feet trailing a sharp line through the moonlit dew. 'I *will* find you!' he said.

Arthur was confused. What did Gabriel mean by 'I *will* find you'? They were standing right in front of him! He waited for the knife to come slicing through the night air. Yaz's hand gripping his made no difference to the terror in his gut.

The fingers of both of Arthur's hands tingled suddenly. It reminded him of a time when he was little and he'd touched the electrified fence that ran round a field of cows. The electric shock had not been dangerous, but it had made him jump. It felt the same now. He dragged his eyes away from Gabriel and glanced at Yaz – or rather, at where he knew she was standing. He could feel the tight grip of her hand, but Yaz wasn't there. She had vanished into thin air! Arthur looked down at his own feet. What the …? They too had gone walkies! Where on earth was he?

No! He wanted to scream, *We've turned into ghosts!* Which meant that Gabriel had already killed them. But then why was Gabriel standing right next to them with a puzzled look on his face? If Arthur was now a spirit, he reasoned, his own body should be lying on the ground. He looked down. The grass was covered in a patchwork of silvery spider webs. No corpses of a boy and a girl. He stared back at Gabriel, smelling the toffee sweetness of his breath. The blades in his hands were not dripping with blood. It made no sense.

Gabriel leaned forward and peered right through Arthur towards the bushes at the end of the lawn. He sighed deeply and turned away, stepping carefully across the grass towards the other side of the house. He looked back once, then disappeared out of sight round the corner.

The moment Gabriel had gone, Arthur let go of Yaz's hand.

'What happened?' Yaz whispered. She pinched the skin on her arm. 'A second ago I wasn't here!'

'Me neither!' said Arthur.

'No. Seriously. My legs, arms, every bit of me, vanished! See-through. And you too!'

'I know. Saved us though.'

'What did?'

'I don't get it. Sounds crazy, but it had to be my dad's arrow. Weird. And it passed through me to you. But whatever it was, he's gone now – and we need to do the same.'

They sprinted across the lawn into the safety of the bushes. A short while later, they scrambled over the wall, panting with relief as they headed back towards Yaz's cottage.

'Next time you wake me up in the middle of the night,' hissed Yaz, 'remind me not to go off on suicidal missions with you!'

'You wouldn't have missed it for the world!' Now they'd done it, Arthur forgot his terror and felt almost light-headed. 'We took on the both of them – and won!'

'For now,' warned Yaz. 'And what makes you think they won't come after us?'

'We'll worry about that tomorrow.'

'And that arrow of your dad's. Did it really turn us invisible?' Yaz shuddered.

Arthur remembered Gabriel's eyes looking through him, as if he were a pane of glass. 'It did something. Who knows? But look – we're not far from your place now.' He slowed his pace. 'Er, are you OK?'

Yaz had stopped and was leaning heavily against a gate. 'My shoulder!' she said. 'It's been aching all evening.

Now it really hurts.' She blinked a couple of times, trying to focus. 'Just want to be back in bed. Need to get home.'

'I'll walk you there.'

'No. I'm fine. I need to sneak in by myself.' She took a few deep breaths. 'See you at school. We'll talk then. Go!'

Arthur backed away, very unsure about leaving her. But, with a determined look, Yaz waved him away.

The walk from the edge of the village usually only took her a few minutes, but Yaz's feet felt heavy. The trees on each side of the lane had turned the way back into an endless, dark tunnel. By the time she reached the side door of the cottage, her lungs were heaving. Each time she moved her shoulder, she winced in pain.

Keys. Lock. Keep quiet. Avoid creaks on stairs. Bit by bit, she dragged herself into her room. Her sister was still asleep and everything appeared normal. But the fire in her shoulder told her otherwise.

Tiredness took hold. She couldn't even be bothered to get changed. She pushed the pillows to one side and collapsed on to the mattress. And that was when it started. Instead of sinking into welcome sleep, Yaz felt as though she was being burned alive. Sweat poured from every pore of her body, soaking her clothes and turning the duvet and sheets into a wet tangle. She moaned with the pain, convinced that the cat was in the room with her, tossing her body from one paw to the other like a juggling ball.

Her cries woke her sister, and her father and mother came rushing in. As they turned on the light, the sight that greeted them was shocking. Their daughter was writhing in bed like an animal, teeth chattering, arms trying to push away invisible enemies. When her mother grabbed a thermometer and pushed it between stiff lips, the temperature was off the scale.

All this time, Yaz was only half present. She didn't recognize her mum and dad and tried to shove them away, muttering gibberish about *green eyes* and *flying arrows* and *knives cutting rivers of blood*.

The doctor was called. This time, she was unable to reassure them. She pushed Yaz gently on to her side and peeled away the bandages. A stench of pus filled the room and the wound was purple and yellow, with thick, swollen tracks where the claws had gouged in. The doctor cleaned the wound, changed the dressing and gave Yaz an injection. She motioned Yaz's parents outside the room.

'The fever is serious,' she said. 'But I want to hold off calling an ambulance. Let's let the antibiotics work a little first. For now, keep your daughter under observation and call my mobile if she gets any worse. Try to keep her cool with cold flannels.'

'Will she be all right, doctor?' asked Yaz's mum.

Doctor Evans put on her best reassuring smile. 'Modern medicine is marvellous stuff, Mrs Mitchell. Let the antibiotics do their job, and I'll be back in the morning.'

Doctor Evans pushed her bag into the car and started up the engine. She was worried, very worried indeed.

CHAPTER 14

Wednesday, one day before midsummer

The phone woke him. Arthur jolted upright, hearing his mum talking downstairs. His head was thumping. Why had he even bothered taking the risk of getting the arrow? It wasn't as if it would bring his dad back.

There was a knock on his door. 'You'll be late, Artie. It's nearly eight. That was Yaz's mum.'

Arthur shot out of bed and wrenched open the door. 'Is she OK?' He could tell something was wrong by the frown on her face.

'That scratch of hers has turned nasty. She's running a bad fever. If it doesn't settle, they'll have to take her to hospital.'

Arthur suddenly felt cold inside. *That damn cat!* He'd already lost his father. He wasn't going to let anything happen to his mate. 'I'll sort it,' he muttered.

'Since when have you been an expert doctor?' his mother sighed. He could tell she'd been crying. And not about Yaz.

'I mean, I'll sort out going to see her after school …' But Arthur had other plans.

His opportunity came at lunch. The sun was scorching, already turning the school into an oven. Those with any sense were outside in the school field, grabbing whatever bit of breeze or shade they could.

He'd seen Jack Mytton in passing at break. The boy was moving at a slow pace as if he was half-asleep. And when they'd crossed each other's paths in the crowded corridor, his green eyes had stared at Arthur with pure hatred.

You don't scare me! Arthur had told himself, forcing himself to believe it was true.

Now, with everyone outside, the corridor was empty and Arthur spotted Jack going into the boys' loos. He took a deep breath. It was broad daylight. So far the *beast* had only come out at night. Arthur hoped that daytime made a difference.

Warily, he pushed open the door. The smell was, as always, disgusting. There was one thing he could never work about boys and school loos. Why was their aim so rubbish? It didn't take skill to hit the spot. And flushing once in a while might be nice too. He tried not to breathe in. The place appeared to be empty, apart from the usual dried-up splodges of loo-roll decorating the walls and ceiling.

'There you are!' came the low voice that Arthur knew so well.

Arthur spun round. How did the boy do that? One moment, there was only light and shadow. The next, Jack Mytton stood lounging against the far wall.

'Something tells me a little thief has been in our house and stolen what was ours.' Jack paused and licked the back of his hand with a darting tongue.

Arthur felt his confidence leak away. He should have brought a weapon. But all he had was words. 'Thieves steal. In fact, that's what your high and mighty father did. He stole what belonged to my dad. I took it back. By the way, the cat food nice and tasty, was it?'

Jack gave a hiss that was half-human, half-animal. 'Think you're clever, boy? And now here we are, all alone. Trickery will not save you this time. I suggest you give it back.'

Arthur could see the muscles rippling under Jack's clothes. 'You *suggest*! Well, you can take your suggestions and shove them where the sun forgets to shine. Messing about with my father's stuff – and now Yaz is ill, thanks to you!' Arthur knew he was taking on a boy who was built like a bull, but he was furious and beyond caring.

Arthur clenched his fists, and anger drove him forward. His arm pulled back ready to strike. One good punch and Mytton's nose would be smashed sideways. But all his fist found was thin air.

Jack had already ducked down, reading the move easily. 'Is that the best you've got?' he taunted, jumping up and using both hands to flick Arthur backwards until he slammed into the opposite wall. 'Though your sense of honour is rather fetching!'

Arthur felt the pain as his head slammed against concrete. He slumped to the floor, the room spinning round him.

'As for your friend's little scratch...' Jack paused and inspected his long fingernails. 'Yes, I'm afraid such a gift comes with a price. It won't be long now.'

Arthur tried to get his breath. He'd come in here to confront Jack. Now the tables were turned. 'What ... what do you mean?'

'The infection will spread throughout her body.' Jack smiled nastily. 'If you want all the gory details, let me lay them out for you. Her skin will be covered in pus and boils. Some will burst, leaving a rather *interesting* perfume. It will be her body fighting against the poison. But the battle is hopeless. She will sweat herself dry and then her heart will be squeezed so tight it will burst in a bloom of blood!' Jack licked his lips, savouring every detail. 'Not a nice death, I admit, but very colourful.'

Arthur curled up against the wall, holding his hands over his ears. This was his best mate that Jack was talking about! 'Why? Why do this to us? What harm did we do to you?'

'Harm?' Jack snarled. 'It was *your* ancestors who trapped us with their goodly spells.' He advanced on Arthur, pointing his finger like a dagger. 'Your ancestors who would happily have locked us in a tomb of rock for all the years to come. My imprisoned mistress has suffered enough. It is only a matter of hours now. Tomorrow morning at midsummer dawn, *She* shall be free at last. The death of you and your stupid little friend are merely a taste of what is to come!'

Arthur stared, horrified. He wasn't sure if Jack was boy or beast. The air shimmered, black uniform turning to black fur, teeth stretching themselves out and shoes thickening into paws.

'And you dare to call us thieves, when all our power was stolen! I should have killed you back on the Stiperstones. But now I'll let you live for a few seconds longer, the time it takes you to hand over the arrow in your pocket.'

Arthur crouched on the stinking floor. 'I … I haven't got it!'

However, for Jack, all games were over. A hand – or was it a claw? – reached out and gripped Arthur round his neck. His body slid upwards, Jack's sheer strength lifting him until he was suspended in mid-air. 'I think you do!' Jack growled.

Arthur couldn't breathe. What a way to go. His namesake King Arthur would have chosen the glory of dying on the field in battle. But Arthur Hatfield was about to kick the bucket in the boys' toilets of his own school. Squitty was not the word.

CHAPTER 15

Arthur's legs dangled mid-air. His windpipe was being squeezed and his eyes were beginning to bulge.

'Can't … breathe!' he gasped.

'Yes,' sneered Jack. 'That is the point.' He tightened his grip on Arthur's throat. 'Now give me the arrow before I snap your flimsy neck in half.'

Arthur had no choice. If he gave the arrow to Jack, he would die. If he didn't, he would … die. It wasn't good either way. 'Let … me … down. I'll give it … to … you!' Each word scraped out of his throat with an effort.

'Very well, but no tricks, boy.' Still holding Arthur's neck tightly, Jack lowered him to the ground. 'Put your hand in your pocket slowly and pull it out.'

Arthur was glad to be standing on his own two feet again. His neck was already one massive bruise. He wished he had a weapon. His eyes nervously scanned the toilets, looking for anything that could help, but he doubted that Jack could be taken on by a couple of loo rolls. No. All that he had was the arrow.

The arrow! Last night, it had made him and Yaz vanish. He could do the same now! Brilliant! But the moment he thought of it, dismay set in. Jack still had his fingers firmly round Arthur's neck. The beastly boy didn't need to see his enemy to crush the life out of him.

However, as Arthur feebly pulled the arrow from his pocket and was about to hand it over, hope flared through his veins. His great-great-grandma might be long dead, but her advice lived on. He suddenly found himself speaking aloud the words he'd found in the shoe. Weird. The words just floated out in front of him: *'Keep the golden arrow safe. It is both key and lock and, in the hands of those with right on their side, it is a … burning spear.'*

'Really?' said Jack. 'You think some old spell is going to save you?'

But Arthur saw a tiny prickle of doubt in Jack's green eyes.

'Not a spell,' Arthur replied, 'but a spear.'

'No trickery, I said!' There was foam at the edge of Jack's mouth. His fingers squeezed tighter, tight enough to stop the pulsing of blood.

With the tiny arrow firmly gripped between forefinger and thumb, Arthur swept his arm up. *This is for Yaz!* Arthur screamed silently as he plunged the arrow into the back of Jack's hand. He knew he didn't stand a chance. A pinprick would hardly stop that same hand strangling him. Or would it?

'Owwww!' Jack screeched. His hand was alight! Blue flames crackled round the fingertips. The point where the arrow punctured his skin pulsated with pure pain.

Instantly, Arthur was free, though he still gripped the arrow. He gasped a lungful of air. Never had a toilet smelled so sweet in all his life. He stared in fascination at Jack Mytton. The part of him that lived as a cat had gone, leaving only a schoolboy howling in agony. Arthur knew he had to act fast and without mercy. He dug the arrow in harder, pushing the sharp point deep into the back of Jack's hand until it burst through veins and grated against bone.

'It hurts!' Jack whimpered like a kitten. Now he was the one on the floor while Arthur towered over him.

'Good!' said Arthur. 'Or as you put it so well earlier, that's the *point*.'

The flames should have burned Jack's fingers to a crisp, but instead they played up and down the boy's arm, causing him agony.

'Now,' Arthur continued, 'as I mentioned before, my best mate is ill because of you. I do hope there's a cure.'

Jack looked up with defiance. 'Too late for that, boy!' he snarled.

Arthur twisted the arrow round, watching as the blue flames raced up Jack's arm towards his chest. 'Tell me, or so help me, I will dig out your heart!' It was so strange. Holding the slender arrow, Arthur felt like a warrior, not a Year Eight pupil during his lunch-break. The arrow spoke through him. Being gentle was not on the cards. 'Answer my question!' he commanded through gritted teeth.

Jack raised his free hand and pointed at the wall above the urinals. 'Have your answer!' he spat.

Arthur watched in fascination as black writing scribbled over the plaster, made by some invisible pen.

**Drink from the well,
undo the spell.
Eat of the tree,
healing of thee.
My cousin stands tall,
silver my shawl.
Shade and light,
a whispering fight.
From death to life,
mending strife.
Devil's claw
will touch no more.**

While still gripping Jack's hand, Arthur read the words aloud. 'A riddle? How the hell does that help?'

'I am bound to do what you ask! The arrow compels me!' Jack cried. 'So this is the answer I give you. And may Hell find you and that infernal girl!' Jack shuddered once. His eyes grew filmy, then slowly closed.

'Mytton! Wake up!' Arthur used his free hand to slap the boy's face. Nothing. Jack's cheeks felt cold. He ripped the arrow out with a tearing slurp. A small trail of purple blood trickled from the tiny wound and the flames around Jack's arm and hand snuffed out like a candle.

The door to the toilets slammed open. Arthur looked up. It was Mr Jeffries, the headteacher, eyes widening in shock as he took in the scene.

'Arthur Hatfield!' he roared. 'What on earth have you done?'

'He attacked me, sir!' Arthur alone knew that he was telling the truth. But the truth was that he didn't know if Jack Mytton was alive or dead.

CHAPTER 16

Arthur jumped up and ran straight towards the headmaster.

'What the devil are you doing, boy?'

There was no time to answer as Arthur ducked under his arm and through the door.

'Come back here!' Mr Jeffries shouted, his voice booming down the corridor.

Arthur had lost his father. His mate was possibly dying and now it looked like he was a murderer. He slammed through the swing doors and into the baking afternoon, running for his life through the school field and over the stile into the fields beyond. He had no idea where he was going. He simply had to get away.

No one stopped him as he sprinted along the footpaths out of town and headed up the valley. Fear pushed him on and sweat turned his school shirt damp. He ignored the brambles ripping his trousers and the high nettles brushing his bare arms. All he could think of was Jack's cold face.

A shrill mewing sound disturbed his thoughts. He looked up into the blue sky. A buzzard circled high overhead. Once the bird had Arthur's attention, it veered off to the west.

Arthur paused to catch his breath. Could it be the same bird? The last time, it had given Arthur a golden gift of hope. The ring still lay deep in his pocket, like a secret. He hadn't even shown it to his mum.

'I must be going crazy. You want me to follow?' he said aloud to the hills around him. This felt stupid. How could a buzzard help him? He shrugged his shoulders. He was in such big trouble; he didn't know what else to do.

The bird hovered briefly, seeming to check that the boy was on course, then flapped its wings and was off again. Following the bird was strangely easy. It seemed as if the buzzard was reading the fields below like a map and leading him onwards. Arthur followed blindly, not really caring where he was being led. His head was too full of terrible thoughts that he wanted to blot out.

Half an hour later, Arthur scrambled and fell over a crumbling moss-covered stone wall. He was in a graveyard by an abandoned church that had seen better days. Headstones leaned at topsy-turvy angles and the grass between them was waist high.

Arthur lay where he had fallen. He couldn't move. He was covered in scratches, his head was pounding and his mouth was dry. He watched the buzzard land in a tall tree that reared up in the far corner of the graveyard. The sun and soft breeze had a strange effect on the leaves. They were like silver coins flipping over and over and each of them made an odd whispering sound.

He wanted to close his eyes. He wanted everything to be normal again. Most of all, he wanted to know what to do.

He stared at the tree and the buzzard stared straight back at him.

'Oh!' gasped Arthur and the hairs on the back of his hand stood up. He knew where he was. He remembered that tall tree from years ago, when he was little. There had been a big celebration and re-enactment of old village customs. Part of it had been held right here, under that very tree. There was a well there. He remembered having to lie on the stony ground, pretending to be dead, while the other children danced round him. Each carried a spoon to splash some of the holy well water over him. Next they sprinkled a pinch of dried-up bark on his clothes because the black poplar tree that protected the well was said to have the power of healing. Then he'd had to leap up when they had finished and say:

'*From death to life,* She *shall not have me!*'

As a kid, it had all seemed a bit of fun. Now, it could be a lot more serious. Jack's riddle might actually make some sort of sense. Arthur looked up towards the tree. The buzzard had gone. In its place was a plan. Arthur just had to hope that the strange writing on the wall really did give an answer to how he could save Yaz. *Drink from the well, undo the spell …*

He jumped up and headed towards the well. Under the shade of the branches, the water was cool and inviting. Arthur needed something to carry water in. He looked around and spotted an old cola can among the leaves. It would have to do. He snatched it up and leaned over the edge of the well to rinse it out. Then he filled it up and balanced it carefully on a stone.

Now it was the turn of the tree. What had Jack's riddle said?

Eat of the tree, healing of thee …

Arthur used his fingernails to prise off a small piece of bark from the black poplar and slipped it into his pocket. He was tired and suddenly thirsty. He leaned back against the roots and took a swig from the can. The water cooled his parched and bruised throat as thoughts swam round his head. Would the police be looking for him? What about his mother? He was exhausted, his head heavy. What could he do next? What could he …?

Arthur came to, feeling knobbly roots sticking into his back. What on earth had happened? He rubbed his eyes. The light had changed. How could it be dusk already? Had he fallen asleep or passed out? He'd wasted hours. This was terrible; he had to get to Yaz as soon as possible. What if he was already too late?

He tried to clear his head. First things first. Jack hadn't wanted him to solve the riddle. But he had. So, Yaz first. The rest could come later. Though, even as Arthur refilled the can, Jack and Gabriel's talk about midsummer dawn came back to him: how 'it' would all be over by then. And the midsummer dawn was now only hours away.

Arthur strode through the graveyard, working out the quickest way to Yaz's house. The low light caught one of the gravestones and the inscribed name stopped him dead in his tracks. *Hatfield*. He didn't have time to stop now, but how could he ignore his own surname? Quickly, he knelt and tore away the ivy that was strangling the headstone. The carved letters were encrusted with years of dirt, but there was the first name: *Clara*.

He felt a lump in his throat. Here was his great-great-grandma's last resting place. Time had forgotten her. This was the woman who had sealed a piece of paper in a shoe. And there, right underneath, sharp as the day it was carved over a hundred years ago, was a message:

Do Not Wake the Devil.

CHAPTER 17

Getting through the village without being seen felt like a living nightmare to Arthur. He wished he'd chosen the longer way round to Yaz's place instead. All the happy houses with normal life going on inside made him feel like a ghost. The light was on in his own kitchen window, drawing him like a moth. He expected to see a police car outside, but there was only his mum's ancient Micra. He knew he shouldn't, but he tiptoed quickly up to the side of the kitchen window and peered in.

It was that man again, infecting the house with his fake smiles. Arthur's stomach churned. Gabriel Mytton was nursing a tumbler of whisky in his hand. Arthur's mum sat on the other side of the table, laughing at something. Snatches of conversation drifted through the open window.

'Boys will be boys!' Gabriel laughed. 'Luckily, my son only had slight concussion, though it would be good to hear Arthur's side of the story. I'm sure he'll be back soon.'

Mrs Hatfield smiled apologetically at her visitor. 'I'm so sorry, Gabe. Yes, no doubt he'll be home shortly; it's getting dark. Arthur can be a bit headstrong sometimes …'

Headstrong? If only his mum knew what was really happening. Arthur felt both relieved and panicky. It was good that the Mytton boy was alive and good that his Mum didn't seem too worried about where he was. But now Gabriel was here, waiting for Arthur to walk in. Gabriel, who last night had carried a pair of blades in his hands. Gabriel, who obviously had his mother under a spell and was now waiting for him.

Arthur felt torn in half. Part of him wanted to go charging in, protect his mother from the man's lies. Would she be safe if he left her there? He had to hope so. It wasn't his mother that Gabriel was interested in. The can in Arthur's hand and the crumbly bit of bark in his pocket reminded him that he had absolutely no choice but to leave and go on. He crept around the corner of the house, reached in the back door and craftily unhooked his rucksack from the peg. He knew there were a couple of torches in it, and he hoped there'd be something to eat as well.

Ten minutes later, he was peering in at another window, at the back of Yaz's house. There was a sofa-bed in the downstairs study. On top of it was a figure. The sheets were thrown off and the light of the desk-lamp showed a face covered in sweat and a red swelling on her neck. There wasn't a moment to lose. Luckily, the window was open to catch the breeze. Arthur gently lifted the latch and climbed in.

Yaz moaned as her body tossed and turned on the bed. 'They're coming! *She's* coming … I can't …'

Arthur crossed the floor, listening out for the sounds of her parents. In the next room, a TV blared. He knelt down, lifted the can towards her lips and said urgently, 'Yaz. You need to drink this!'

Her eyelids fluttered and opened. She didn't even seem to see him, but grabbed his shoulders. '*She's* coming!'

Arthur recoiled from the foul stench of Yaz's breath.

'Don't worry,' Arthur said soothingly. He tried cradling her head with one hand and tipping the can towards her mouth. 'Just a couple of sips.' The water dribbled down her cheeks, but some of it made its way past her clenched lips. 'Good. Well done.'

Now came the hard part. Arthur took out the piece of bark and snapped off a tiny flake. He crumbled it in the palm of his hand and added a drop of water to make a paste. 'Open wide,' he said, using the point of his finger to try to drop the paste into her mouth.

Yaz suddenly gasped and her jaw shot open. As a dollop of the bark mix went in, she swallowed, then coughed loudly. Arthur turned towards the door, expecting her mother or father to run in. What exactly would he say? *Hello, Tahira. I found a cure by beating up a boy who is a cat in his spare time. Then I followed a buzzard to a church graveyard and gathered the ingredients to try some sort of old magic on your daughter …*

Yaz closed her eyes and her body went limp.

Arthur waited. It was hopeless. Some stagnant water from a cola can and a stupid bit of bark. Jack had lied to him. Or, even worse, this would speed up the sickness. He held his head in his hands.

'Art … Artie?' The voice was faint. 'Is that you?'

Arthur looked up. 'Yaz?'

'Feel weird. Been ill.' The glaze in her eyes had gone and sweat was beginning to dry on her brown skin.

Arthur couldn't believe it. It had worked! 'And some!' he said. 'Got to you just in the nick of time.'

'Thirsty …' Yaz tried to sit up. 'Had a bad dream.'

'Drink some more water.' Arthur grabbed a pillow from the bottom of the bed and helped to prop her up.

The well water had an amazing effect. Colour returned to Yaz's cheeks immediately and her voice became clearer. 'What happened to me? Where have you been?'

Arthur sat at the edge of the sofa-bed and began to tell his story.

'So the writing just appeared on the wall?' Yaz asked blearily a few minutes later.

'Yeah. And now it makes total sense. *Drink from the well, undo the spell. Eat of the tree, healing of thee.* Jack never thought I'd work it out.'

'I wish you had killed him!' Yaz said.

'Yeah. But I didn't fancy the long prison sentence. Anyway, I have to get back to that church tonight.'

Yaz yawned and sank back into the pillows. 'Why?'

'I found my great-great-grandma's gravestone. There was some writing on it. *Do Not Wake the Devil.* I need to find out more. It's midsummer morning at sunrise tomorrow …' Even as he spoke the words aloud, the room changed. A draught ruffled the curtains at the window and Yaz's eyes widened.

The hum of the TV in the next room suddenly died. Footsteps approached the door. 'Shall I check up on her, love?' Yaz's dad.

Arthur froze. It was mad. If there was anyone he could trust, it would be Yaz's parents. But there was too much to explain.

The voice of her mother came through the door. 'No. Let her sleep.'

Yaz put her finger to her lips and leaned over towards Arthur. 'Those words,' she whispered. 'I've heard them before. They were in my dream while I was ill … the only thing is it was too late. I felt something reach towards me from deep underground. And that something was definitely a *She*. And that *She* has been asleep for ages, but now, well, *She*'s waking up. In my dream, her fingers pushed through the earth like worms and her fingernails were so sharp …' Yaz trembled as the dream came back to her. Then she shook herself. 'So, I guess this means we're off again. Where are my trainers? What about when my mum comes and checks on me? If I've gone, they'll have the police out.'

'You are *not* going anywhere!' Arthur stared at Yaz and shook his head. 'You're staying right where you are.'

'I'm coming with you,' Yaz said firmly. 'If you say no, then I'll call Mum and Dad in right now and tell them everything. Besides –' she reached over and drank the rest of the water in the can – 'I feel totally fine now.' She was already out of bed and standing up. 'See? No problem. Completely better. Right, I'll stuff a bunch of pillows under the duvet and turn the light off. Hopefully they'll think I'm still sleeping. Anyway, seems to me that's the least of our worries right now. OK. Ladies first.'

And with that, Yaz slipped over the windowsill and outside. 'Are you coming or what?'

CHAPTER 18

Half an hour later, they stood outside the church. The building was different by moonlight, filled with dark edges and uneasy shadows.

'My legs are wobbly,' Yaz admitted, leaning against the door frame.

'Here,' said Arthur, pulling a banana out of his bag. 'Instant energy.' He didn't say what he was really thinking: that he was worried she was too weak to be there.

'What are we looking for?' she asked between bites.

'I don't know,' Arthur said. 'The truth?'

They'd already looked at Clara's gravestone. But there was nothing else to see.

Yaz still looked pale and shaky. 'What now?'

The great oak door at the back of the church porch was locked. 'Mmm,' Arthur replied. 'Shine the torch on the ground, under the bench.'

She did as he asked. There was a brick in the corner and poking out from under it, a rusty old iron key.

'How did you know?' asked Yaz.

'Not sure,' Arthur replied, fingering the arrow in his pocket. 'It felt right.'

He put the key in the lock and turned it with a scraping sound. The door was jammed shut though. The torch beam picked out cobwebs strung all the way round the frame with dead flies wrapped in silver thread. Nobody had been here for years.

Arthur put his shoulder to the door and heaved. With a creaking groan, it finally gave way. Inside was a palace of shifting shadows. The moon shone through the stained glass, sending fingers of light to pierce the gloom.

Yaz pointed the torch upwards. A huge old oak beam crossed the front from one wall to another. On top of it was a plaster wall filled with old writing. Arthur tried to read the words. 'Thou shalt not … kill.'

He remembered the sudden hardness inside him as he had dug the arrow into Jack's hand. Anything could have happened.

'Here!' said Yaz. 'I think I've found something.'

Most of the church was whitewashed, but in the far corner a faded painting had been left visible on the wall. The light from the torch picked out gruesome details. The rolling hills were pretty enough, but the cave mouth at the centre was a black hole. Beneath that, naked bodies tumbled down into a cavern filled with flames. The tiny humans screamed silently as they were boiled alive or cut in half by demons with pitchforks. Watching from the side, on a throne of molten lava, sat a figure. Her dress was made of human skulls. A forked tail wagged behind her like a dog. But it was the expression on her face that was the worst. The painter had caught the figure's utter delight at all the suffering around her. By her side stood an angel with black, charred wings and in her lap curled a creature that looked like an eel with fangs.

'Gross!' said Yaz.

There was a plaque next to the picture. It told how builders in the 1930s had been putting in electric lights when they uncovered the painting, along with a Latin description.

'It's been translated,' Arthur said, as he continued reading:

This picture shows an old Shropshire folk tale called 'Do Not Wake the Devil'. Shown here, the Devil takes female form. We see her tempting one of the heavenly angels with promises of eternal power if he will help to defeat God. According to the tale, Archangel Gabriel fell for these promises and together they nearly succeeded in their plot.

'Gabriel?' said Yaz.

'It can't be! This is only a story.' Arthur turned back to the plaque.

'It was then that our legendary hero King Arthur played his part.'

'Hey!' said Yaz, 'Is that you then?'

'Sssh,' said Arthur. 'There's more.'

The king took his knights with him deep down into the caves under the

> Stiperstones. And there, with the Lord's
> help, they found the gateway to Hell and
> defeated the She-devil. She had a servant
> with her that could take the shape of all
> animals but who went mostly in the form
> of a black panther. This foul creature was
> slain.

Arthur shook his head. Although he knew the story was wrong about that last bit, the pieces of the puzzle were all fitting together.

> They bound the She-devil with chains
> of gold washed in holy well water. For
> Gabriel, the punishment was this: his
> wings were hacked off with an axe and
> he was made to wander the earth for all
> eternity. From then on, he was known as
> Dark-angel Gabriel.

Arthur thought of Gabriel Mytton in his bedroom, the horrible scars on his back. Could it really be?

He continued reading.

> Arthur and his knights then made the
> greatest sacrifice. It is often told that they
> sleep deep underground, round their
> table and wake only in times of war. But
> in this version of the tale it is their sleep,
> their holy and good dreams, that binds the
> She-devil and keeps her power chained.
> Thus, once a year, before the midsummer

dawn, the good knights must be taken a feast, else the sleepers will grow weak and the Devil awake again. Of course, this is an old myth and only of interest to the curious ...

'No it isn't!' said Yaz.

'Listen. I'm not finished.' Arthur bit his lip.

According to the story, there was one family who was entrusted to look after the sleepers. A small golden arrow was forged to be carried by them as a symbol of trust between the knights and their protectors. But it was also the most sacred of weapons, only ever to be used if all else was lost.

Arthur pulled out the arrow from his pocket, seeing it glint under the torchlight. The myth had come to life. It lay in his palm.

'It's all true!' Yaz said in wonder. 'And my dreams were part of... Ahhhh!' She lurched sideways suddenly. 'What was *that*?'

'Whoa!' Arthur grabbed her elbow as the ground rippled beneath their feet. Up above, a crack zigzagged between the commandments. One of the glass windows shattered and the shards rained down.

'We have to get out!' Yaz screamed as the old stone walls of the church began to shake. 'I don't know what's happening and I don't think I want to know. Just go!'

CHAPTER 19

The wooden pews rocked backwards and forward, and the walls trembled like sheets of paper. The sound was dreadful, as if every stone in the church was screaming.

Arthur reached the door first. He grabbed the great iron ring and pulled, but nothing happened.

'It's no good!' he shouted above the noise. 'The door's jammed. I can't shift it.'

They cowered in the corner, feeling the ground move under their feet. It was as if the earth was coming to life.

'*She*'s waking up, I'm sure of it,' Yaz shouted into Arthur's ear.

But at the same moment, the shaking stopped. There were creaks and sighs of settling stone and toppled wooden pews. A breeze blew in through one of the broken windows, swirling the clouds of dust that were floating through the moonbeams. The silence was heavy.

Yaz stood up nervously and peered around. 'Maybe *She*'s like a cat, playing with us.'

Arthur didn't answer. He was trying to remember his last lesson with Mr Stockheart. 'Or maybe … it was an earthquake.'

'You what? In Shropshire?' Yaz said.

'Yes. Right here. Right now. It's not the first time.' He stood up shakily and tried the door again. This time, he was able to heave it open. The sight of the dark sky outside was a huge relief.

Yaz pushed past him. 'Remind me never to go to church in the middle of the night with you ever again!'

'Righto.' Arthur shrugged. He had a nasty feeling that this was only the beginning.

The gravestones nearest the door were in an even worse state than before. It was as if someone had come along with a massive ten-pin bowling ball and knocked them all over. They had to pick their way through carefully.

'Earthquake, you reckon?' said Yaz.

'Well, I don't like the other explanation, do you?'

Yaz shook her head. 'You're right. Doesn't bear thinking about.' She gripped Arthur's arm suddenly. 'The village! Our homes? What if anyone's been hurt?'

'Look around you. What do you see?'

The full moon showed that only part of the graveyard was affected. All the stones at the far corners were fine, as well as the surrounding wall.

'It doesn't make sense!' exclaimed Yaz.

'Could be a landslip right under the church,' Arthur suggested. 'These hills are riddled with old mines.'

'Whatever it was, we were dead lucky,' said Yaz. 'What do we do now?'

Arthur looked at the glowing face of his watch. 'It's less than six hours until the sun rises. Jack and Gabriel both kept talking about midsummer dawn, and now the story in the church confirms it too.'

'And, according to you, the sleepers haven't been fed since your great-granddad's time,' said Yaz.

'Yeah. Well, I've got a couple of apples in my rucksack.'

'And I've got an idea! Back in a minute.' Yaz turned round and ran back into the church. When she appeared again a moment later, she was grinning.

'What was that all about?'

'Later. Do you know which mine it was? The one where they used to leave the food?'

'I'm sure I can find it. It's near the quarry where my dad …' Arthur frowned. He could feel tears pressing behind his eyes. Here he was, off on a wild goose chase and he hadn't even thought about his father.

'OK,' Yaz said slowly. 'Then that's where we should go.'

As they made for the gate out of the graveyard, there was one last surprise waiting for them.

A large slice of broken stone blocked their path. They were about to climb over it when Yaz peered closer. 'It's a gravestone cover! It's been shifted from that grave there. Look …' She pointed. Next to the path was a deep, stone-sided pit. The force of the tremors had lifted the great covering slab as if it had been a piece of cardboard and heaved it sideways. Leaning forward at an angle above the open grave stood the stone statue of an angel. The face was covered in bird droppings, but under the moon it looked like blank eyes were weeping blood. Yaz flicked her torch over the inscription at the angel's feet.

GABRIEL MYTTON, 1835–1872.
MAY HIS SOUL FLY IN PEACE.

'Must be one of his ancestors.' Arthur shuddered. 'He told us his family came from round here.'

Yaz shook her head. 'No, think about the story. Anyway, how do you explain that?' She moved the torch beam so it shone into the pit. 'Empty!'

Arthur peered down into the darkness. 'Maybe the coffin got thrown about too.'

'It's always been empty,' Yaz said matter-of-factly. 'He never died, did he?'

The hole in the ground stared back at them. It was somehow magnetic, pulling them forward. Arthur thought that it would be so easy to just climb in and lie down.

'Urghh!' said Yaz. 'It gives me the creeps. C'mon. Let's make a move. Now.'

Arthur shook himself. She was right. They'd got what they came for: information. Though he didn't like where it was leading them.

'Aren't we getting a bit out of our depth here?' Arthur began as they left the graveyard. 'Perhaps we should let the police deal with this?'

Yaz didn't agree. 'Brilliant, Artie. Two kids turn up in the middle of the night to tell the local PC that the She-devil is having a nap beneath the Stiperstones. She's being guarded by King Arthur's sleeping knights, who need to be fed before dawn. And, by the way, if they don't have some nosh, she'll wake up and all hell will break loose … Yes, I can see that all going down a treat.'

'Well, I guess, when you put it like that!' Arthur found himself smiling grimly.

'I do. It really does seem that you're the last of the guardians. So it's up to you. I'm just the dumb mate who's come along for the ride.' Yaz sighed. 'Mind you, you'd only muck things up without me. So, are you up for doing the job your family was given – before the sun rises?'

'Do I have a choice?'

'No.'

Arthur and Yaz fell into silence, walking as fast as they could. Arthur knew that the time for talking had gone. It was what lay ahead that filled him with fear.

CHAPTER 20

'Is this it?' Yaz asked.

They had reached the top of a sloping field of heather and fern. In front of them was a dark opening just over a metre high, fringed with curtains of ivy. Far above, a single mass of stone reared up on the horizon, clenched like a giant fist. It was known locally as the Nipstone.

'Yeah,' said Arthur. 'Weird to think there was once a whole village here.'

'Where?'

Arthur waved his arm towards tumbling piles of stones further down the hill. 'Gone. Engine houses, mine-workers' cottages. My granddad said this place was buzzing when his dad was a kid.'

Now, it was quiet, apart from the endless drip-drip of water leaking through the roof of the mineshaft.

Yaz felt her dizziness returning. She pushed aside the ivy and pointed her torch inside. The stone tunnel was rough, hacked out by pick-axes. There were tiny white stalactites hanging from the ceiling like dead fingers poking through. 'How do you know this is the right place?'

'The name: Lordshill. It has to be it. Plus, my granddad brought me here when I was little. I'm sure this is where he told me his dad and the other villagers used to leave food.' Arthur was also aware that the arrow was growing hotter in his pocket. He pulled out a second torch from his rucksack, grabbed one more gulp of fresh night air, then plunged past Yaz and bent double to begin creeping down the passage.

Yaz stood at the edge, unsure.

'Only two things to worry about!' Arthur called back. 'Roof-collapse and flooding.'

'Is that all?'

'Yeah. At the moment. We can worry about other stuff later.' His voice trailed off. He didn't want to think about *later*.

Yaz took a last look behind her and clambered into the tunnel mouth. 'Wait for me.'

Inside, the ground was covered in a few of inches of black water, hiding hollows and holes. It was slow going for the first hundred paces or so, but gradually the roof rose until they could stand up. Then the tunnel split into two. One path was dry. The stream they were paddling through rushed into the tunnel on the right.

'Er …' Arthur stopped. His hand crept down towards the arrow in his pocket. 'I'll check this one first. You wait here.' He splashed away into the darkness of the right-hand tunnel.

'Yeah. It's this way,' he called back. 'Watch your feet though. Ow!' There was a sudden echoing splash.

Yaz leapt into the tunnel, wading through the water as it reached above her knees. 'Artie! Where are you?' Her torch beam showed the current of water flowing past her, filling the tunnel floor completely. Ahead, everything widened out. There was no sign of him.

'Artie!' she screamed.

She moved her foot to step forward, but couldn't feel anything underneath. Instead, she flung herself backwards, then she shone her torch down. She was standing on a submerged lip of rock. Beyond it the ground dropped away into deep water. She waved the thin beam of torchlight across the surface – still nothing. She bit down hard on her bottom lip and tried again. Something caught her eye. It was a pale hand clawing its way up out of the depths. Yaz couldn't move. She stared in horrified fascination as a second hand emerged and scrabbled against the tunnel wall. It was followed by a head, with bulging, bloodshot eyes – Arthur's! She heard him gasp and splutter as he grabbed hold of jutting rocks, then he was hauling himself up and out, no more than five metres away.

'That is seriously c-cold!' he puffed, shivering on a narrow ledge.

Yaz was so relieved to see him that all she could think of to say was, 'What happened to your torch?'

'Dropped it. Sorry. Bit of a shock the tunnel floor disappearing like that. Shine yours over this way. Look, this ledge carries on. You can climb up on to it.'

Yaz splashed over to the side of the tunnel, clamped her torch between her teeth and felt carefully with her feet. It was wet and slippery, but there were plenty of handholds. Arthur waited for her to reach him, then together they scuttled sideways like crabs until they reached a water-filled cavern.

There was a fluttering far above them. Yaz trained her torch upwards. A thousand pairs of beady red eyes stared back at her.

'Bats!' she said.

'Who's bats? You or me? Actually, we both are!' Arthur joked, trying to lift the tension, but it didn't work. His mouth was dry and his wet clothes were making him shiver. 'Come on!' Arthur continued inching his way along. 'Once we get round this cave bit, I think the water gets more shallow.'

He was right. Soon the ledge turned into a wider path running around the lake rim. As they reached the other side, they could see rocky ground under the water. However, they could also see where the water was going: straight over the edge of a sheer drop.

The roar grew louder as the cave narrowed again and the lake turned into a waterfall. The path came to a dead end. They peered over the edge, watching the torrent thunder down into a dark hole.

'No way down!' Arthur shouted. 'What now?'

'Are you sure it's that way? Can't we go back and try a different tunnel?'

Arthur didn't need to put his hand into his pocket to feel the arrow pulling him on. It was like a burning magnet, dragging him forward. 'I just know this is the only way. We have to manage it somehow.'

Yaz sighed and pointed her torch beam along the edges of the crashing waterfall. She was just about to tell Arthur it was impossible when the light caught a tiny jutting step carved into the rock, and another below it.

Although she couldn't see all the way down, it looked as though there might be enough rock steps and handholds to give them a good start.

This time Yaz insisted on going first. 'Hold my hand and don't let me fall.' She used her free hand to hold the torch and guide their way as she climbed down on to the first step. Her toe slid around on the slime, but finally her foot found its grip. 'Take it slow. We should be fine.'

Arthur braced himself. The sound of the waterfall was deafening and he had no idea what was at the bottom or even how far down they would get. But all he had to think about was one step at a time. And, with each step, the arrow was pulling them deeper into the heart of the hill.

'How nice to see you!' A voice sang horribly above the crash of water.

Arthur looked up. The darkness above them was suddenly lit up and a glowing figure stood at the top.

'And just in time to bring back what was needed!'

Arthur panicked. His numb fingers lost their grip and his feet scrabbled helplessly against the rock. He slithered down, landing on Yaz and knocking the torch from her hand.

'Artie!' Yaz screamed and they both tumbled straight down.

CHAPTER 21

Yaz woke first. She was lying on something gritty but soft. She groaned in pain and opened her eyes.

There was a dim light that meant she could see. Up above, the rock cliff reared steeply. The waterfall veered off to her right, rushing down into another sheer tunnel. She was on a bed of sand, thinking that they were lucky to have had this soft landing instead of being washed away. Arthur lay a few metres from her and was beginning to stir. Yaz moved her head to look to her left. 'What the …?'

'*What the devil?* is the phrase I think you are looking for. Very apt too.'

Gabriel Mytton was standing on a flat slab of white crystal rock. The tidy black suit he wore looked odd against the surroundings.

Yaz peered at the slab again. This was the source of the strange, luminous light. It revealed a cavern the size of a hall. Yaz could neither move nor think properly. She was still trying to work out why they hadn't fallen all the way down with the waterfall.

'Ah yes.' Gabriel seemed to answer her question. 'There are huge cracks in these deep shafts that can easily swallow a river. The water is now somewhere far below us. As are the sleepers. And you have so very kindly brought me the key!' Gabriel stepped off the slab and knelt by Arthur's side.

'Leave him alone!' Yaz croaked.

'It's too late for that, I'm afraid.' Gabriel dragged the groggy Arthur towards the slab, flopping his body over the edge. 'Come. You might as well see what the arrow is truly for!'

Despite herself, Yaz slowly managed to stand and staggered towards the slab. It was a perfectly flat rectangle about the size of a door.

'Your thoughts are right for once. This is a door!' Gabriel smiled. In his hand, he now held the tiny arrow that shimmered like a firefly. 'I am so glad that Arthur decided to join us here. It needs a *righteous hand* to hold the arrow, or should I say – key. Otherwise it won't work. Of course, I could always just chop it off, but a severed hand might not work so well.' He took the arrow and curled Arthur's fingers round it, then forced the boy's hand towards the surface of the slab.

The moment the arrow touched the white rock, there was a sudden flare of flames. A booming clap resounded in the cavern. The whole slab slowly shifted to the left, hidden hinges grinding round.

Gabriel kicked Arthur's arm away. 'My dark dream has come to life finally,' he sighed. 'Before I say goodbye, would you like to see what lies below?' He pointed into the gaping hole revealed by the slab. There were steps leading down. 'After you!' he said and gave a mock bow.

Yaz staggered over to Arthur and helped him to his feet. 'Are you all right?'

'My head hurts,' Arthur mumbled. 'But I'll live ...'

'Not for much longer!' Gabriel sneered. 'Now in you go!' He herded them down the wide, pale crystal steps beneath the slab. At the bottom they found themselves in a vaulted hall the size of a cathedral. It was carved from the same white rock, warm and filled with the sound of snuffling breath.

Arthur and Yaz gazed around in shock. It was a story come to life. In the middle of the hall stood a huge, round table and circling it, twelve seated knights. However, their armour was not shining but rusted. And the bodies inside the chain mail were as gaunt as skeletons, shrouded in cobwebs. Their chests rose and fell in the thin rhythm of uneasy sleep. The thirteenth chair held a king. But his crown had slipped sideways over a face wrinkled with the centuries.

'Behold your sleepers and their sad old king! It really is a pity that you stopped believing in the ancient customs. These so-called holy guardians have not been fed for a hundred years or more!' Gabriel stalked round the table. 'How easy it would be to bring their dreams to an end.' He whipped out a knife and, in one easy motion, slit the throat of one of the knights. There was an awful gurgle as a thin line of blood appeared on the sleeper's neck. The knight slumped over.

The chamber shook. A sound like a deep sigh rose from below.

Yaz screamed and backed away.

Arthur felt sick. 'What was that sound?'

'Do you really need to ask? I thought you had done your research. Dawn will come soon and it won't just be the sun waking up! *She* will wake too.'

Arthur looked down. The stone slabs beneath his feet shifted slightly, as if he was standing on a boat.

'Do you not know how heavy the earth is? Flying in your pathetic human aeroplanes is not even an echo of riding the currents of air.' Gabriel wiped the blade on his sleeve. '*She* has promised me my wings again. What more could an angel desire?' The blade glittered dangerously in his pale hand.

'You're sick!' Arthur spat.

'Yes,' Gabriel admitted. 'And I shall be made whole again!' There was a flash of light and the blade in his hand swooped once more, piercing straight through chain mail. A second knight breathed a last rattling breath. The round table shook and frowns appeared on the faces of the remaining sleepers. 'One by one! Each dream is a chain that can be cut.' Gabriel paused to look down at Yaz and Arthur. 'You humans with your greed have already helped Her wriggle from her coffin. Famine, wars and the rising tide of pollution – all this is food for Her nightmares. Believe me, we shall rule!'

Arthur toppled sideways as a crack appeared and widened in the floor beneath him. The heat rising from the depths was like a furnace.

'Ahhh,' Gabriel murmured. 'It is *She*!' He fell to his knees.

Something crept up out of the blackness below. It uncoiled very slowly, like a rope twisted out of dark smoke.

Then five shapes fanned out from the end, taking the form of a hand. Arthur tried to scrabble backwards, but he wasn't fast enough. The fingers uncurled and reached straight for him, closing round his ankle.

A sound rose again. This time, it was a hissing whisper. 'Sooo hhhuuungry!' it shuddered.

Steam poured off Arthur's wet trousers and a fierce, burning pain filled his leg. 'Help!' he screamed.

Yaz stood, petrified as Arthur was slowly dragged towards the gaping hole in the floor.

Gabriel looked up from where he was kneeling. 'I have done what was asked, my lady. Each life I lay before you shall make a soup of blood to quench your thirst!' He rose with blade held forward, ready to continue its dreadful work.

Arthur locked eyes hopelessly with Yaz. 'I'm sorry!' he whimpered. 'We've failed. It's over.'

CHAPTER 22

Arthur struggled against the evil force pulling him over the edge of the chasm, his feet dangling right over the edge. Gabriel watched, his eyes glittering.

Yaz, still frozen in horror, stared too. But her mind was racing and, as thoughts whirled around her head, she found herself reaching into her pocket. Her hand clutched a packet. It was what she had run back into the church to find earlier, just after the earthquake. She had taken it from behind the altar. Its contents were stale, but she thrust her hand in and pulled out several crumbling wafers: holy communion wafers. Crushing them in her fist, she darted towards the hole in the ground and flung the tiny flakes at the twisted hand shape. A shower of sparks exploded and fizzled, and the smoky outline of the hand turned to white vapour. Steam writhed and curled, and Arthur was suddenly released as the smoke slithered back into the darkness.

Arthur scrabbled to haul himself away from the edge.

Yaz spun round to face Gabriel. She saw his stunned face and backed away from him towards the knights around the table. She bumped against the shoulder of a still-sleeping knight. His mouth was half open, breathing softly. Keeping her eyes on Gabriel, Yaz grabbed a handful of wafers from her pocket and crammed them straight into the knight's mouth.

'Eat!' she shouted. The knight didn't stir.

'Communion wafers. Oh, how clever!' Gabriel said. He had recovered from his shock and was now on the opposite side of the table. 'You think a few bits of blessed biscuit will do the trick?' He stalked round towards Yaz, holding his knife straight towards her.

'It already did! Arthur's still here, isn't he?' said Yaz defiantly.

'A few flakes may have bought you some mere moments of time. But *She* will still rise!' As if in answer, the ground again trembled beneath their feet. 'Now come, child. Better to give up your silly games!'

'We'll see.' Yaz grabbed the chin of another knight, forced open his lips and sprinkled in another handful of broken wafer.

'I told you,' Gabriel snarled, 'they have not been fed for a hundred years. Your stale crumbs will make no difference.' Then he paused. 'What was that?'

'The answer to my prayers!' Yaz whispered as the first knight's lips began to move. At first it was no more than a dry cough. Then two distinct words.

'I … wake!'

Eyelids flickered open to reveal eyes, clear and blue as the midsummer sky.

The effect was astonishing. Cobwebs and dust slid off the knight's body and rust peeled away from the sword at his side. The wooden chair on which he sat was pushed back. The knight stood up for the first time in a century. He swayed briefly, before turning to Yaz and giving a small bow. Then he swivelled round and fixed his bright eyes on Gabriel.

For the first time, Gabriel looked worried. Suddenly, his knife was a tiny toy compared with the sharp length of steel now brandished by the knight. As the knight stepped forward, Yaz was in a frenzy, running round the table, pushing wafers into sleeping mouths.

'I wake!' boomed another voice. And another. And another. Finally, it was the king's turn. As he rose from a deep sleep, Yaz saw that his crown was made not of metal but of polished antlers. He stood slowly, taller than all his men, taking in the scene and his two dead companions.

The king's knights drew up behind him as he faced Gabriel. He took a deep breath and his eyes were filled with both sorrow and anger.

'What is this?' the king roared. 'Was it not enough that we cut your wings and let you live?'

It was Gabriel's turn to be rooted to the spot. 'Why did I kill only two of you?' he squeaked. 'I should have done away with the lot of you while I had the chance.'

The king pulled his sword from his side and raised it high. '*Chance* is something you have wasted. And now it is time for you to pay dearly. Come, men, take up arms!' His voice filled the cavern as sword blades sliced the air.

'Mistress! Help me!' Gabriel shrieked in terror. But the knights advanced, closing around the Dark-angel Gabriel. Their swords shone like lanterns.

'Give me mercy!' Gabriel begged, falling to his knees.

'Mercy?' cried the king. 'Is that what you showed my fellows here and these brave children?' He pointed to Yaz, and to Arthur, who was dragging himself upright. 'We have been woken and fed, and now it is time for us to feed you – a sharp meal of justice.'

Gabriel tried to fling up his arms to cover his head. But as the word *justice* echoed, the king's sword swooped down, straight through his throat. For a moment, Gabriel hung as though suspended in the air, a look of pure amazement frozen on his face. Then, one by one, the knights lifted their arms and thrust their blades into his slumped body.

Arthur could hardly bear to watch. He almost felt pity for the poor, wingless being. But as the body took blow after blow, he stared in fascination. Instead of blood, plumes of dust billowed out from the wounds. The last knight brought down his sword, but when he lifted it again, all that remained were tattered rags of clothing. Everything that had been Gabriel was gone.

Yaz moved to Arthur's side. Silence settled with the dust. Then the king stepped forward and stood before them.

'You are the keeper?' he said to Arthur. And Arthur nodded as he felt the burning of the arrow in his palm where he was still clutching it. 'And you, my lady,' the King said, turning to Yaz, 'you have done well. Such holy food will keep us for another year.'

Yaz smiled. *Feed the sleepers.* That's what she'd done.

The king continued. 'But now we have woken and fed, we must to sleep once more, else the crack in the floor shall grow large.' He glanced behind him. 'If the custom is forgot again, there is no hope for the world.' He looked directly at Arthur and Yaz in turn. 'It is up to the young who still believe that all things are possible. Else this earth will burn to ash ...'

'We'll come back, every year!' Arthur said. 'We promise. And next time we'll leave you proper food.'

'Good.' The king swept round. He nodded to his men to return to the table. But as they moved away, the steps leading to the cavern above filled suddenly with an agonized, yowling hiss and a shadow of black fur.

All eyes turned in alarm to see the cat. Arthur stared in horror. The last time he had seen Jack in cat form, he had been the size of a panther. Something had happened. Perhaps it was Jack Mytton's anger at Gabriel's loss that had shifted and twisted his shape. Or perhaps it was because he was now so close to his mistress, but he had grown to the height of an elephant and the claws that sprung forward made the knights' swords look like matchsticks.

The massive beast charged, intent on ripping everyone to shreds.

CHAPTER 23

The king and the knights raised their swords to face this new danger.

'Defend!' shouted the king.

But already the cat was among them, scattering the men like skittles. One brave knight darted behind the slashing claws and tried to stab the cat in its soft underbelly. He pushed the blade in deep, expecting the huge animal to be fatally wounded. There was a trickle of blood, but nothing more.

The cat reared up, until the man was hanging by the handle of his sword, a surprised look on his face.

'A tiny pin!' it hissed. 'Pathetic! It is a mere scratch.'

With one swing of a mighty paw, the knight and his sword were ripped free. The cat's claw skewered the man straight through his guts and out the other side. There was a brief pause as the cat considered what to do with its victim. The knight screamed in agony as his intestines slipped free from the rip in his stomach. He was impaled on the claw, wriggling like a worm on a hook.

'Pah,' the cat spat as it tossed the body aside. The knight flew through the air and slammed with a sickening crunch against the far wall of the cavern. Dead.

'One … by … one!' rasped the cat, turning to face the others. 'In memory of my master Gabriel and for *She* who will not be stopped.'

The knights had backed against the table, looking to their king for orders. The king stepped in front of them and rested the tip of his sword on the stone floor.

'You are nothing but a conjured ghost!' he shouted, his voice shaking the rock. 'No more than a foul thought from the deeps!'

'Really?' The cat sat, its green eyes flickering, and licked the blood from its claw.

'Yes! And I command you to go!' The king lowered his head so that the sharp antlers on his crown faced forward. And he charged.

The cat reared up on to its hind legs as the antler crown pounded into its thigh and the king's sword sliced across the fur of its belly. It gave a sharp hiss of pain then pounced down, swatting the king sideways with a huge paw.

'Is that small graze the best you can do?' hissed the cat. 'A forgotten king and his sad old knights! The midsummer dawn is nearly here. It is time!' The cat narrowed its eyes and looked around, its gaze falling on Arthur. 'Come, mistress. Let us feast together!'

Once again the ground shook. And again an intense heat rose up as the chasm grew wider. Slowly, so slowly, twisted fingers crept up and over the edge.

The knights, Yaz and Arthur were trapped. Burning depths on one side. On the other, the prowling brute.

117

The king pulled himself upright and stood still, gripping the hilt of his sword. His eyes searched out Arthur's. 'The arrow!' he whispered. 'In the last, it is also the most sacred of weapons, only to be used if all else is lost.'

Arthur had read the same words before, back in the church. And the arrow was gripped tightly in his hand. Gabriel had made a mistake using it only as a key to enter the chamber. But Arthur had no idea what to do now. In the boys' toilets, he had been able to grab the boy Jack and stab his hand. He looked up at the enormous beast towering over them. He had no chance of getting close enough to use it without having his face ripped off.

'You are the guardian. You will know what to do,' the king commanded, staring deep into Arthur's eyes. 'As shall I.'

With that, the king strode forward to face the animal, holding the hilt of his sword steady with both hands. 'I challenge you!' he cried. 'You shall not pass!'

The cat threw back its head and laughed. Then, pulling in its mighty shoulders, it sprang towards the king.

Arthur had no time to think, but two words from Clara Hatfield's note filled his head: *burning spear*. As if with a will of its own, his arm swung up, his wrist flicked back like a whip and the tiny arrow flew straight towards the beast.

The moment the arrow left his hand, everything slowed down. The knights and Yaz watched in awe as the arrow stretched and grew. It was golden elastic. Instead of something the length of a matchstick, what flew through the smoky air towards the creature was a spear. Flames shimmered along its length to a razor point – sharper than a sun-flare.

The king needed only to step out of the way as the gold spear plunged deep into its target – the cat's eye.

There was a yowl of agony as the big creature staggered backwards. It scrabbled with its paws, trying to pluck out the blinding torment.

Arthur's mouth hung open in amazement. Black fur briefly rippled, then began to turn grey as the cat toppled sideways.

'You … *you* have beaten me. How …?' it croaked.

Before everyone's eyes, the beast that had been about to kill them changed. The terrifying creature cowered and gradually, from tail to head, it turned to stone. One last whimper, and Jack-the-cat was completely still, a lump of rock.

Arthur knew he should have felt pleased, or at least a grim satisfaction. Everyone was staring at him. He watched the king's mouth open and close and realized he couldn't hear anything for a roaring sound in his ears. Then his feet left the ground as fingers closed tightly round his neck.

Through bulging eyes, he could just make out the arm snaking out of the chasm. But this time, the burnt, smoke-woven hand squeezing his throat was not letting go.

CHAPTER 24

The finger and thumb were a noose, crushing the air from him. Arthur choked. The smell made him want to gag. His eyes stared helplessly and the cavern spun round him.

Arthur thought about the so-called Myttons, Gabriel and Jack. What could he do? They had been kittens compared with this. Now his only weapon was gone, while this enemy was growing in strength moment by moment. The cave floor shuddered. Splinters of rock and crystal fell from the ceiling. He couldn't breathe. In fact, he could barely see. He was dimly aware of the king striding forward with a grim look. His royal sword swung through the air, straight towards Arthur. Perhaps it was better this way: to be killed with mercy by the good king. It was better than being strangled slowly by the She-devil. Arthur closed his eyes, waiting for the impact.

The sword swept round in a delicate arc. It sliced swiftly in, towards Arthur's neck. There was a shuddering jolt and Arthur was flung to the ground. He landed with a thump and heaved in great lungfuls of air. By his feet, the shape of an amputated thumb twitched. The remaining four fingers writhed at the end of the arm. The king swung his sword again, cutting straight down. The clang of metal on stone rang shrill and the hand was severed. The scream that rose from deep within the chasm almost cracked the walls of the cavern.

'Be gone!' the king roared. 'In the name of all that is green and good!'

The king's command echoed. His warriors moved to his side, blades held high. Each blade shone with a strange light that focused together into a single beam. The light shot down towards the dark hole and the smoky remains coiled back down into its prison, far under the earth.

Screams howled from below. They were unearthly, filled with putrid anger, hate and defeat. One by one, the knights lowered their blades, still pointing into the deep, and advanced, shoulder to shoulder, until the tips of their swords rested at the very edge. The cries began to fade. There was a gigantic clap, and the crack in the ground slammed shut. All that was left was a plume of smoke that quickly thinned, then was gone.

The hall was silent. The king turned slowly to look around. The table was cracked and chairs scattered. Three bodies of knights good and true lay where they had fallen, never to rise again. The furrows in the king's face were deep, his eyes sad.

'The winning of this battle has cost us dear,' he said, sighing. 'Come here, young Arthur. And you too, Yasmeen.'

Both Arthur and Yaz felt exhausted. They were also nervous.

'I'm sorry,' said Arthur. 'I should never have let Gabriel get the arrow …'

'And the whole village let you down,' said Yaz. 'They should never have stopped leaving food for you. People forgot. Nobody believed in you any more.'

The king gazed at them. 'But you did,' he replied, solemnly. 'And your belief was enough.' He looked round at his assembled knights, counting how many were left. 'What is this world when we need the children to save it?' He sighed again, then opened his mouth and yawned.

As he did, the cavern lit up suddenly. A shaft of pink light seeped through a crack in the high roof above them.

'Ah!' the King murmured. 'The dawn approaches. We must return to our slumbers. Come, my good men.'

The knights bowed their heads to Arthur and Yaz and carefully sheathed their swords. They turned towards their chairs.

Arthur looked puzzled. 'Don't you want to be free?'

The king settled into his throne. 'By our being here, all those above are free – until such times as the call comes and we are needed. We must sleep and dream. It is our dreams that bind the one below, that keep *her* chained so she may not wake.' He paused. 'Now go. And remember your promise. A year today, leave more than a few wafers of holy dust. It is a century since we have tasted cheese or cake.' A ghostly smile played across his lips.

'We will,' murmured Yaz. 'A proper feast. That's what you'll get. I might even bring you some of my own samosas!'

'Before you leave us,' the king mumbled, his lips now barely moving as sleep began to claim him, 'there is an easier way out.'

His eyes flicked to his left. The shaft of dawn light had revealed a second set of steps, almost hidden among a tumble of rocks at the far end of the cavern.

'You shall find a gift waiting for you. The underground rivers brought us something. Trust me, your prayers will be answered.'

'I don't understand,' said Arthur. 'What do you mean?'

It was too late. The king and each remaining knight sank deep into their chairs and closed their eyes. Soon the cavern was filled with the sound of soft, deep breathing.

'That's it then,' said Yaz.

'But what about the knights who were killed?'

As if in answer, the three slumped knights stood up. Or appeared to. Yaz and Arthur rubbed their eyes. The bodies still lay in the same places. What rose up had the same shape, but these other figures were see-through. Their faces shone as they slowly drifted towards the shaft of light.

Yaz and Arthur felt no fear, for there was no terror about these spirits. Each figure paused before them, kneeling as he crossed his hands over his chest. There was no need for words. They were grateful, forever.

The figures stood straight and proud. One by one, they stepped into the thin beam of sunlight. Like sugar in tea, they dissolved. Yaz and Arthur were alone again. They took one last look at the sleeping knights and stumbled towards the other steps. As they began to climb, they heard a grinding sound behind them. They didn't need to turn around to know the stone had slid into place, sealing the cavern once more.

CHAPTER 25

Thursday, midsummer dawn

'Look!' Yaz gazed ahead.

The sight was wonderful. A circle of daylight grew larger as they hurried up the tunnel. This time, there had been no waterfalls or dangerous currents that dragged them under, just an endless set of steps rising from deep underground. Their calves were aching, but it was worth it.

A few minutes later, they scrabbled on hands and knees through the tiny gorse-covered opening.

'Oh, wow!' Arthur paused to catch his breath. The sun was just above the horizon and mist spread through the valleys. 'We're out! We're alive!' He sank down among the white rocks and scree.

Yaz too flung herself down on the white rocks of the Stiperstones, soaking up the early rays of sunlight. 'It feels so different.'

'Weird to think it's a school day.'

'Yeah. It's unreal. From taking on … all that back there to going to … geography. Well, not for me though. I'm ill at home, in bed, remember! Or I was last time anyone looked in on me.'

'What now?' said Arthur.

'Home. Creep back into bed before anyone's up. Shower. Breakfast. Normal stuff. I'm really looking forward to *normal*.'

'What do we tell our families?'

Yaz frowned. 'Not sure. No one will ever believe the truth.' She stood up and began to pick her way over the tumble of white stones. 'Maybe nothing at all. Better that way.'

'Strange to think of that lot down there, dreaming away.' Arthur nodded back towards the hidden entrance.

'Yeah. Good, though. Keeping us safe and all that.'

'I suppose,' said Arthur. 'Unless *we* dreamt the whole thing.'

'Yeah, right. Check your pocket.'

Arthur did. He gasped as he pulled out the arrow, now returned to its usual size. 'But ... how? And how did you know?'

'I didn't,' said Yaz. 'But you're the Hatfield guardian, remember. And I'm sure the king doesn't want us to forget ever again!'

'Good point. And now that we're talking of feeding the sleepers, I could murder a bacon sarnie!'

'Now you're talking!'

Yaz ran ahead. The Stiperstones were soon behind them, the sharp ridge standing out across the sky. The path ahead dipped down between high hedges then curled into the valley, leading towards the old quarry. Far above, they could hear the mewing call of a buzzard. It reminded Arthur of something.

They crossed a clearing and skirted the edge of the pool. On the far side, a moorhen fussed over her chicks as they bobbed into the water. Arthur had the sudden urge to jump in too. He wanted to cleanse himself of last night's events. Then he remembered the buzzard and the gold ring that was still in his other pocket. He thought of what he'd truly lost.

'All that we did,' he muttered, hurling himself down on the ground and hunching over, 'but it still won't bring him back.' He stared angrily into the water.

Yaz carried on, not seeing that Arthur had stopped. She turned a corner, out of sight.

Arthur heard a scream. No! Not again. Not after everything else. Yaz was screaming his name. 'Artie! Artie! Artie!' Over and over. He raced and stumbled towards her shouts, bursting round the bushy thicket. His legs almost gave way as he began to take in the sight in front of him. His head whirled. This couldn't be happening.

Yaz was crouching over something blocking the path. Something large, curled up and pale.

Arthur threw himself forward. Hope and despair flared in his chest. He was sobbing so hard he could hardly get out the words: 'Dad! Dad!'

The curled figure lay on its side, wearing only a pair of swimming trunks. Nothing else, except the dawn dew beaded on his skin.

'Dad! Dad!' Arthur croaked again, kneeling down and reaching forward with shaking hands. The fear was almost too much. What if he was stone cold? What if …? His fingers touched his father's face. The skin was soft … and warm.

The body stirred, groaned. Eyes opened. 'Art ... Artie, is ... that ... you?' The words were slurred, sounding as though he was speaking underwater.

'Yeah. It's me. Here ...' Arthur tried to help his dad sit upright. He pinched himself. He didn't want this to be a dream.

His father looked round, his eyes trying to focus. 'Hello, Yaz,' he said.

'Er, hi, Mr Hatfield. Are you all right?'

Arthur's dad scratched his wet hair, pulling out twigs and leaves. 'Think so. Bit cold.' He paused. 'I was having a lovely swim. Dusk. Can't beat it. Me and the buzzards in the sky above and the sound of skylarks. And then ...' He frowned. 'I suddenly felt ever so heavy. Something pulling at me, dragging me down and wrapping me round with words. Sick words, all about killing and wars and poison. She had a horrible voice ...' He broke into an embarrassed smile. 'I must sound like I'm going mad!'

'No, you don't at all, Dad.' Arthur wanted to keep holding on to him, keep feeling how real he was. Had *She* really pulled him down into the deeps?

'Then I was dreaming. I felt my skin shrivelling up in the heat, being burnt alive, but I couldn't die. And the voice again, screeching that the last of the guardians of the arrow *must* die – so that she could be free. Weird. Then this huge bloke with antlers on his head turned up. He was carrying some hefty-looking chains and he was angry. Dead angry, but not with me ... Next thing I know, Yaz here is yelling fit to burst and you're here.' He turned to look at his son. 'Funny what tricks your mind plays. Must have been something I ate. I guess I must have swum back to the edge of the pool and then passed out. What do you think?'

'Something like that, Dad. Just glad to have you back. Me and Mum were …' Arthur had no idea how to explain. His father had been gone for a month. And as for all the other stuff? He didn't know where to begin. 'Well, anyway, best get you home first, eh? We can talk later.'

'Grand idea, son. Could do with a nice hot cuppa.'

Ed Hatfield tried to stand up and nearly fell over. Yaz and Arthur supported him, one each side. Slowly, as daylight beat away the shadows of the night, they moved down through the valley and towards the village.

CHAPTER 26

A year later, midsummer eve

'Pork pies! Is that the best you can do?' said Yaz. 'Good job I brought something too.'

They sat down for a breather, halfway up the Stiperstones. Clouds drifted over the crescent moon high up above.

'Give me a chance. That's just the first course. I also managed to bake my first ever batch of winberry pies. Told my mum it was for a school project!' Arthur knelt down and rearranged the plastic boxes in his rucksack. 'Are you sure it's round here?'

'Well, we're not far from the tunnel we went in by. And your granddad told you that was where the food used to be left. But I reckon they won't be battling up waterfalls to get their feast. Makes sense they'll use the same way out that we did.' Yaz swung her torch round, trying to find the hidden entrance into the guardians' chamber. 'Now, which gorse bush was it?'

'What if none of it existed at all?'

'Artie. We've been through this a million times. The police were all over the Myttons' place, wondering where they'd vanished to.'

'True,' said Arthur, remembering the endless interviews. 'Glad we didn't try to tell them the real story. They'd have locked us up.'

'Exactly. It doesn't matter that nobody else will ever believe us. And how did they explain your dad going missing for a month? Amnesia? Yeah, right.' She shone the beam in Arthur's face. 'So, no, we didn't imagine the whole thing. It happened.' She reached up and rubbed her shoulder. 'You know, some nights I still wake up, feeling those scars on my shoulder hot and itchy'.

Arthur jolted round in fear. 'Did you hear that?' he whispered.

'What?' said Yaz.

'Growling. Like a tiger or something.'

Yaz punched Arthur's arm. But her heart missed a beat. 'Scaredy cat! Since when did Shropshire have shape-shifting pumas called Jack Mytton, eh?' She looked round nervously. 'He did die, didn't he?'

'Straight through the eye and right into the brain,' Arthur replied. He remembered the anger in his heart as he had thrown the arrow. He reached into his pocket and felt its comforting shape. It was so strange how it had returned to him. He knew now that for the rest of his life he would carry the arrow with him always. He shivered and looked around. 'Over there,' he said, pointing. 'I reckon it's behind that pile of stones.'

Arthur emptied his rucksack: crisps, coke, leftover cake from his mum's café job, pork pies and winberry pies. He remembered his great-great-grandma's written words. *Feed the sleepers.* He hoped she'd be proud.

'And here's mine,' said Yaz. 'Samosas and bhajis and naan bread.'

Together, Yaz and Arthur laid out the food on paper plates and stood back.

There were no cats to disturb the night, no dark angels stalking in the shadows. And as the moon grew pale and hung from the edge of the world, Yaz and Arthur picked their way downhill, leaving their offerings for the waking sleepers to find.

Far below, the sleeping knights began to stir. Deeper still, *She* who had dreamed of waking still slumbered in chains of dark, uneasy sleep. *She* would not wake.

Stone Circles and Scary Beasts

By Christopher Edge

Exploring the myths on the moors

Stonehenge. An ancient circle of stones that has stood in the west of England for thousands of years. But who built it? And why?

Many people have different ideas about why Stonehenge was built. Some ideas are stranger than others! Some people think Stonehenge was:

- a temple built to worship the sun;
- a clock telling when to plant and harvest crops;
- a graveyard;
- an intergalactic alien spaceship car-park!

How did they do it?

Whoever built Stonehenge thousands of years ago must have been strong. In the centre of the stone circle, ten stone pillars stood over six metres high. On top of each pair of pillars, a huge slab of stone was placed to make a doorway. These huge slabs of stone weighed nearly fifty tonnes each .

Nobody knows how people living thousands of years ago would have managed to lift these into place. Even today, we would have to use heavy machinery to do this. But this isn't the only mystery about the stones at Stonehenge.

Some of the huge stones used to build Stonehenge were brought from a quarry in Wales, over 150 miles away. The people who built Stonehenge managed to move the stones all that way before they even had roads. When a modern-day team tried to recreate the stones' journey using wooden rollers, they failed; the stone ended up at the bottom of a river. No wonder some people still think the builders of Stonehenge used magic to make it!

Merlin's magic circle

According to one legend, the stone circle at Stonehenge originally came from Ireland, where it had been built by giants. The magical stones had special powers that could heal people. When King Arthur's magician, Merlin, was ordered to bring the stones to England, he used magic to fly them across the Irish Sea. He then built the famous circle at Stonehenge.

Don't count the stones

If Merlin did build Stonehenge, then maybe some of the magic he used to move the stones is still there. Old tales say that a magical spell cast on Stonehenge means that nobody is able to correctly count the number of stones that are there. Each time you try, you come up with a different number. Legend has it that anyone who breaks the spell and correctly counts the stones will die!

Down with the dead

Stonehenge isn't the only place where legend says that death is close at hand. The West Kennet Long Barrow is a huge prehistoric tomb. Inside the barrow, over forty skeletons have been found.

At dawn on Midsummer's Day, the ghostly figure of a man has been seen entering the tomb. He is shadowed by a white dog with red ears and glowing eyes. Some say this dog is a hellhound and anyone who sees it will soon die themselves!

Turned into stone

White Moor Stone Circle stands in a lonely corner of Dartmoor in Devon. Local legends say that the nineteen stones used to be a huntsman and his dogs. They were turned into stone by a bolt of lightning as punishment for hunting on a Sunday. Some say that at night you can hear the howls of the dogs from inside the stones.

Spooky dogs

The ghost dog at West Kennet Long Barrow isn't the only ghostly hound that is said to haunt Great Britain.

• **Black Shuck**: According to the legends of East Anglia, this gigantic black dog has one red glowing eye. It can be seen at night on lonely country lanes following foolish travellers. If you feel the icy breath of Black Shuck on the back of your neck, chances are you won't make it home alive.

- **Death Hounds**: The Death Hounds are a whole pack of ghostly black dogs. Known as the Wisht Hounds in Devon, the Dandy Dogs in Cornwall and the Gabriel Hounds in Yorkshire, this ghostly pack of dogs is said to appear on Halloween. They are led by a phantom huntsman and hunt down the souls of the dead. Legend says that if you get in their way, the Death Hounds will tear you to pieces!

- **Bogey Beast**: This ghostly beast can change its shape. Sometimes appearing as a white, yellow or black dog, the Bogey Beast tricks its victims into following it. It then leads them to deep rivers and pools to drown and disappears with a hideous howl.

Beast of Bodmin

Legends of mysterious beasts lurk among the many stone circles that litter the moors of Devon and Cornwall. Giant black cats the size of panthers and pumas have been seen prowling the moors. Are these animals that have escaped from a zoo or a much scarier kind of creature?

In the 1990s, a black panther-like creature was spotted on Bodmin Moor in Cornwall. This creature was named the Beast of Bodmin. When dead bodies of sheep were found on the moor with terrible injuries, farmers blamed the Beast. One person even managed to film the creature.

The British government sent a team to try to find the truth about the Beast, but they weren't able to track the creature down. Even a squad of RAF officers using night-vision goggles couldn't find the Beast. In the end the search was called off and the mystery remains unsolved.

135

So if you fancy exploring the stone circles out on the moors, you might want to take extra care. The Beast might still be out there...

More wild cats

Mysterious big cats have been spotted in other parts of England. These include the:

- Beast of Exmoor
- Beast of Dartmoor
- Surrey Puma.

We would like to thank the following school and students for all their help in developing and trialling *Do Not Wake the Devil*.

Biggar High School, South Lanarkshire

Sean Christie

Andrew Colgan

Daniel Cummings

Nathan Gallant

Aaron Houston

Rachel Inglis

Stephen Lamberton

Struan MacDonald

Katie McAndrew

Isla McLachlan

Darren Riddell

Tiegan Ritchie

Danielle White

David Whitefield